"'

Closi... didn't ...
so...high. But I promised Jason I'd get it down for him."

"Are you afraid of heights?"

"I didn't think so—until now." Lily's tongue darted out to lick her dry lips.

"Want me to help you down?" Devin asked.

"It would be nice."

"What's my reward for saving a damsel in distress?" His eyes glittered as mischievously as her eight-year-old son's.

Liliane shook her head. "What do you mean, your reward? How about just being a good boy and giving me a hand?"

"I'm not a boy—good or otherwise." The sexy smile Devin flashed Lily made her toes curl in her sneakers. "But I'd be delighted to give you my hand."

Danielle Kelly had never intended to become a writer, but her love of books—and romance—eventually led to a writing career. Now she can't imagine doing anything else.

She met her own real-life hero when she was sixteen and married him a few years later. They live in Rialto, California, with their two energetic young daughters, Danielle and Kellie.

To Mom, my biggest fan, and to my husband, Don, who believed in me even when I didn't. This one's for you.

THE FAMILY MAN

Danielle Kelly

W🌐RLDWIDE®

TORONTO • NEW YORK • LONDON
AMSTERDAM • PARIS • SYDNEY • HAMBURG
STOCKHOLM • ATHENS • TOKYO • MILAN
MADRID • WARSAW • BUDAPEST • AUCKLAND

Special thanks and acknowledgment to
Janelle R. Denison

ISBN 0-373-83286-9

THE FAMILY MAN

One

Lilianne Austin stretched out her arm, reaching for her son's kite, tangled in the branch above the one she was perched on. Her fingers came up a good twelve inches short. The elm limb, although sturdy, groaned as she tried inching closer. A cool Colorado spring breeze flirted with her bangs, tickling her forehead.

"You've almost got it, Mom. Just reach a little higher," her eight-year-old son, Jason, instructed from below.

Easier said than done, Lilianne thought as she eyed the Batman kite Jason had so carefully crafted. The plastic casing covering the framework had a Batman emblem on it with strips of white, yellow and black cloth added to the end to make an impressive tail. "I'm trying, Jason," she said, using her legs to slide forward. The bark scratched her bare thighs, making her skin burn. Reaching forward, she realized in disgust that she wasn't any closer to retrieving the kite. Her five-foot-three frame obviously didn't qualify her for kite rescue.

Why had she insisted on saving the kite, anyway? When her son's redheaded friend, Rusty, had offered to climb the tree in her front yard, why hadn't she let him? And where the hell was a man when you needed one? They were so undependable!

"You might have to climb up onto the next branch, Mrs. Austin," Rusty said, squinting up at her.

Lilianne looked down at the freckle-faced boy, intending to tell him she had no intention of climbing any higher, even if it meant abandoning the kite. The ground, seven feet below, loomed up at her, making her stomach pitch recklessly.

"Oh, God," she moaned as she closed her eyes, her head spinning dizzily. She should have known better than to look down. Old fears resurfaced, paralyzing her.

Squeezing her eyes shut, Lilianne willed away the dreadful memory of falling off a ladder as a child, which had resulted in a broken arm. Clutching the thick tree limb with her legs and palms, she forced herself to breathe deeply and remain calm until she regained her equilibrium. She hiccuped.

"Mom, are you okay?" Jason asked worriedly. "You don't look too good."

"I'll..." she croaked, then hiccuped again. She swallowed to ease the dryness in her throat. "I'll be fine. Just give me a, *hic,* minute." Good Lord, what was she going to do? She couldn't depend on Jason to help her out of her predicament. She had scaled the tree easily enough. How hard could it be to get back down?

Drawing a deep breath, she opened her eyes, staring straight ahead.

"You should have let Rusty or me get the kite down, Mom. We're not afraid to climb trees," Jason said.

Rub it in, why don't you? she thought. So she was afraid. Was that such a crime? The hiccups, her body's natural reaction to fear, came more frequently now, shaking her with their force.

"Are you stuck, Mrs. Austin?" Rusty asked guilelessly.

"Of course she's stuck, stupid!" Jason rolled his eyes. "Can't you see she's afraid?"

"I'm not stupid," Rusty said, hands on hips.

"Are too."

"Am not."

"Jason, *hic*, it's not nice to call other people names," Lilianne managed to reprimand.

"Should we call the fire department, Mrs. Austin?" Rusty asked.

Jason snorted. "Firemen rescue kittens out of trees, not people! Jeez, everybody knows that!"

The situation was so ludicrous Lilianne almost laughed out loud, but the thought of losing her balance made her swallow her hysterical giggles. "Boys, I want you to, *hic*, go next door and..." Her voice trailed off as the familiar rumbling sound of a motorcycle reached her ears. Devin, her late husband's best friend, always did have impeccable timing. Her heart flipped in her chest and her body tingled. The flutters were due to her phobia about heights, she assured herself.

Jason, upon hearing the motorcycle, immediately forgot his stranded mother and ran toward the driveway, shouting with glee. Rusty followed him, infected by his boisterous friend's excitement.

"Uncle Devin!" Jason squealed.

Devin McKay pulled his Harley to a stop and switched off the ignition. He turned just in time to catch a flying Jason in his arms. "Hey, there, Tiger," he said affectionately, ruffling the boy's light blond hair. He gave him a squeeze and let him go. Unbuckling his helmet, he got off the bike. "Hi, Rusty," he said to the other boy.

"Hi, Mr. McKay," Rusty answered shyly.

Her fear momentarily forgotten, Lilianne watched through branches and leaves as Devin shoved his fingers through his mahogany hair. It fell in soft, thick waves away from his face. The red T-shirt he wore stretched tautly across his broad shoulders and clung to his flat stomach. Tight jeans, old and faded to a pale blue, revealed incredibly toned buttocks, lean hips and rock-hard thighs. Pulling a baseball card from his T-shirt pocket, he bent toward Jason. The boy's face lighted up with a huge smile, and he threw his arms around Devin's neck. Lilianne's heart constricted and a wave of love washed over her. Devin was so good with Jason and her twelve-year-old twin daughters, Elizabeth and Emily, treating them like his own.

Devin started toward the house, flanked by the boys. "Where's your mom, Jason?" he asked.

Jason stopped in his tracks, his eyes widening at his forgetfulness. "She's stuck in the tree," he blurted.

"She's what?"

"We got Jason's kite tangled in the tree," Rusty informed him, pointing to the large tree in the front yard. "Mrs. Austin climbed up to get it, but now she's afraid to get back down."

Hearing the conversation clearly, Lilianne groaned. Oh, why did Devin have to be the one to rescue her from her foolishness? But she wasn't too proud to accept his help.

"I want to put this card with my collection," Jason said, raptly eyeing the gift Devin had given him. "Want to come with me, Rusty?"

"Yeah." Rusty followed Jason into the house, the kite and Lilianne once again wiped from their little minds.

A smile of amusement tugged at the corners of Devin's mouth as he stared at the large tree. He started forward, his long legs eating up the distance quickly. In a moment he stood directly below Lilianne.

"Hi, Devin." Lilianne gave him a shaky smile.

"Hello, Lily," Devin said, his voice low and husky, almost intimate. The tone he used was the one that made Lilianne's insides melt like warm butter. "Whachadoin'?" he asked, his dark brown eyes glinting with laughter.

Lilianne tried to appear casual, as if sitting in a tree was something she did every day. "Oh, nothing, *hic,* just hanging around."

Devin grinned. Even in her fear she still managed to be feisty, he thought. And incredibly beautiful. She had pulled her reddish gold hair into a ponytail, but a few playful strands had escaped to frame her delicate face. Her eyes, wide and bright, were green, almost an emerald color. She wore a pink blouse and white shorts. His eyes traveled quickly over the length of her, coming to rest on the hands that clutched the tree limb like a lifeline, her knuckles white. A giant hiccup tore from her throat again and her fingers flexed. He frowned, suddenly realizing the seriousness of the situation.

"Lily, are you okay?" he asked gently.

Closing her eyes as her body spasmed with another hiccup, she drew a breath. "I shouldn't have climbed up so high."

"Are you afraid of heights?"

"I didn't think so, *hic,* until now." Her tongue darted out to lick her dry lips. "Remember when I told you I fell off a ladder when I was a little girl?"

"Yeah, I remember," he said grimly.

She smiled sheepishly, her eyes still closed. "Well, I kind of thought about falling off the ladder while I was up here."

"Oh, sweetheart," he said sympathetically, watching as her body jerked with another hiccup. "Why didn't you wait until I got here so I could get the kite down for you?"

One eye peeped open in irritation and glared at him. "How was I supposed to know you were coming over? I'm not telepathic."

Thank goodness she wasn't, Devin thought, because she'd be appalled at the thoughts running through his mind. The way she was bent over the limb made her blouse gape open in front. He didn't think she realized the first button had come undone, allowing him a view of creamy, sloping breasts covered in champagne lace. Every time she hiccuped, they bounced invitingly. He'd often wondered what those soft breasts would feel like in his hands.

Raising his eyes back to her pale face, he concentrated on the matter at hand. Desire coiled low in his body, and unless he controlled the response immediately, he was going to embarrass himself. "I called a while ago, Lily. Didn't Elizabeth tell you I was leaving the body shop early to stop by?"

"No. She's had the phone permanently attached to her ear for the past two hours, *hic,* talking to her girlfriends. I'm surprised you managed to get through." Lilianne shook her head, resolving to buy her daughters their own phone. That she hadn't received Devin's message didn't surprise her.

"Would you like help down?" he asked.

"It would be nice."

"What's my reward for saving a damsel in distress?" Devin's eyes glittered mischievously. Crossing his arms over his chest, he rocked back on his heels.

Lilianne's eyes narrowed. "What do you mean, *hic,* what's your reward? How about being a Boy Scout and doing your one good deed for the day?"

"I've never claimed to be a Boy Scout." The sexy smile Devin flashed Lily made her toes curl in her sneakers. "But in your case, I suppose I can make an exception." He paused a moment, flicking a piece of imaginary lint from his T-shirt. "That is, if you reward me with a nice, hot meal."

"That's blackmail!"

He shrugged. "The way I see it, it's bargaining. You need help out of the tree and I'm hungry. You know what a lousy cook I am."

She really didn't mind his staying for dinner. In fact, she enjoyed his company immensely. She thought of the lonely evening ahead without his presence and answered, "It's a deal."

Devin grinned and stepped forward. Tall and well built, he was an impressive six foot two. All he had to do was reach out and he could grab Lilianne. He placed a large hand on her waist.

"Reach out and put your hand on my shoulder," he told her.

"I, *hic*, can't!"

"Lily," he said in a soft, soothing voice. "I won't let you fall. I'll catch you."

"I . . . I can't," she stammered. Her eyes beseeched him.

Sighing, he leveled his feet apart on the ground, bracing himself for her weight when it came. "Relax, sweetheart. Close your eyes and take a deep breath."

She did as he ordered, letting the tension ease from her body. Without warning, she was hauled from her perch and slid down toward Devin's strong arms. Panicking, she groped for the limb, her anchor, but only succeeded in scraping her backside on a sharp branch protruding from the tree. A loud rip filled the air and a sharp pain shot through her. Strands of hair tangled in the leaves, pulling from her ponytail. Then she was in the safety of Devin's arms, her whole body trembling from the ordeal.

"You're okay, sweetheart." Devin held her body close. "You're just fine."

Lilianne didn't feel fine. She was shaken to the core. "I'm sorry," she murmured against the hollow of his shoulder, her arms wrapped tightly around his neck. "I didn't mean to, *hic*, struggle against you."

"Are you going to be okay?" He carried her toward the house, holding her in his arms as if she weighed no more than a bag of feathers.

She nodded her head. "Yes. My rear end is kind of sore, but you can put me down." She pulled her face away from his shoulder and looked into his chocolate-brown eyes. "Thanks for rescuing me," she said in a soft voice.

"Your welcome," he managed around the thick knot in his throat. He wanted to kiss her so badly he could almost taste her. His eyes fell to her lips, debating. No, he thought. He wouldn't risk their friendship for the sake of a kiss. Because it wouldn't be a chaste kiss. He wanted to taste her lips, wanted to let his tongue explore and tease the depths of her mouth. But a kiss like that would alter their relationship, and he wasn't sure she was ready for that.

"You can put me down," she said again, aware of the sensual spell being woven between the two of them. Her hand suddenly felt warm and tingly where it rested on his chest. She noticed that her other hand stroked the hair curling around the nape of his neck. Abruptly her fingers stopped their foray.

"I want to make sure you aren't hurt." Devin maneuvered the front door open, still keeping her in his arms. Turning sideways, he entered the living room. Finally he set her on her feet.

Lilianne twisted around to check the area on her backside that stung. Seeing the tear in her white shorts, along with a goodly amount of white flesh, her face turned a warm shade of crimson. Her silk panties were torn and she could see a trace of blood.

"Here, let me check that cut for you." Devin touched her arm, intending to turn her around to inspect it.

"No!" She jumped back out of his reach. "I'm fine, really."

"Lilianne, I've got blood on me that's come from you." He stood impatiently, hip cocked to the side. "I want to make sure you don't need stitches."

"I don't."

"How do you know? You can't even see the cut." He took a step toward her.

She took a step back. There was no way she was going to let him investigate the cut on her fanny. It started on her buttock and trailed down the back of her thigh. Even though she couldn't see it well, she could feel the burning, stinging line to know what vicinity it was in.

He sighed. "Lilianne, you're being childish."

"I am not." She stuck out her small chin. "I can take care of my own cuts, thank you very much." With that, she backed out of the room until she couldn't see him any longer. Only then did she turn, keeping her hands covering the gaping hole in her shorts.

Devin grinned. Once he heard her bedroom door close, he followed her down the hallway. He opened her bedroom door without knocking.

Lilianne gasped at the intrusion. She was bent over in front of an oval dressing mirror, trying to examine her wound through the slash in her shorts. She immediately straightened. "What are you doing in here?"

Closing the door, Devin leaned against it. His eyes scanned the room, decorated in soft shades of rose and mint-green. The last time he had seen her room had been about a month before Michael, Lily's husband and his best friend, had died. Then the room had been all beige and blue, far more masculine than feminine. Now, the massive four-poster cherry bed was covered in a rose-colored satin-and-lace bedspread, with frilly pillows tossed against the headboard. A sheer fabric was draped from poster to poster, knotted with silk flowers at the top of each pole.

An antique armoire stood open, and Devin could see Lilianne's clothes and shoes inside. Next to that sat a Victorian dressing table with a hand-stitched cushioned chair. The pastel watercolors on the wall added to the softness of the decor. Lilianne had used her expertise as an interior designer to transform the room into a haven of femininity.

The only trace of Michael that Devin could find was a framed family portrait on Lily's dresser. He thought about the man he'd met when he'd been a freshman in high school, and how they'd become the best of friends. Then Michael had met Lilianne and the three of them had been inseparable. Unfortunately Devin had fallen in love with Lily, even though he always knew she was Michael's girl. Out of respect for Michael and their friendship, he'd kept his feelings for Lily tucked away in his heart all these years.

A tragic car accident had severed Michael from Lily's life nearly three years ago. For the longest time after Michael's death Devin had been torn between his feelings for Lily and his loyalty to the man who had been his best friend. He began to wonder if now was the time to reveal the secret he had kept hidden deep inside him. Was Lily ready for it?

Lilianne's voice finally pierced his reverie. He looked at her, his brows furrowed over his eyes. "What?" he said, knowing she had asked him something, but not at all sure what.

"Devin. You seem a million miles away." She moved away from the mirror, removing her reflection from his view. "I asked you what you were doing in here."

He pushed himself away from the door. "I want to check your cut to make sure you don't need a tetanus shot."

"Shot?" she gulped.

Silently he admitted to being a cad. He knew she hated needles. "Yeah. If it's a deep cut you'll have to get a tetanus shot so you don't get lockjaw."

Her eyes widened and she touched her chin. "Lockjaw?"

"Yeah. But if it's only a scratch we can put an antibiotic on it and you'll be fine. Is it a deep cut?"

Lilianne chewed on her lower lip, absorbing what he'd just told her. What if she needed a tetanus shot? What if she didn't get one and got lockjaw? "I'm, um, not sure."

"And you can't see it properly to be sure," he said reasonably. "Now do I check it out, or do I drag you to the hospital and tell them you need a tetanus shot?"

"You wouldn't!"

His mouth curled into a challenging grin. "Try me."

"You would," she said defeatedly. She resigned herself to his looking at her fanny. Humiliation brought a heated flush to her cheeks.

Devin chucked her lightly under the chin, winking. "It's not like I've never seen a bare butt before, Lily."

She shot him an agitated look. "Yeah, I'm sure you've seen your share."

Flashing his bad-boy grin, he gestured toward the canopied bed. "Get up on the bed and lie down on your stomach."

Grumbling, Lilianne did as he asked, keenly aware of the hole in her shorts and panties showing a patch of inflamed and painful skin. *Quit being a ninny,* she scolded herself. *Think of his examining the cut as a gesture of brotherly concern.* She rolled her eyes. Yeah, right.

Devin sat down on the bed, his hip pressing into her waist as he leaned over and inspected the wound. It wasn't as bad as he'd originally thought. The smeared blood made it seem like a deep gash, but the scratch hadn't penetrated anything more than the surface skin. That diagnosed, he let his eyes linger longer than necessary on the saucy curve of her derriere. His gaze traveled the length of her thighs and firm calves, then back up again. Desire twisted his insides.

"Well?" She lifted herself up on her elbows and looked over her shoulder at him, her ponytail flopping to the side. "What's your diagnosis, Dr. McKay?"

"You're fine," he said, forcing his voice to sound normal. He willed away the heat settling low in his belly. "A little antibiotic cream should take care of it."

Lilianne met his gaze. She saw the desire in his eyes, and a strange, long-forgotten warmth spiraled deep inside her. Shaking off the growing sensation, she slid off the bed, careful not to get any blood on the spread. "I'll go take a shower and make sure it's clean before I put anything on it."

He stood. "Good idea." Devin swallowed his offer to apply the salve for her.

Jason chose that awkward moment to barge into Lilianne's bedroom. "Uncle Devin, are you going to get my kite out of the tree?"

"I—"

Lily cut Devin off. "Jason, what have I told you about knocking before coming into my bedroom?" She and Devin hadn't been doing anything improper, but Jason knew better than to enter her room unannounced.

"I'm sorry, Mom," Jason said, his head hanging. "I didn't think you'd be getting dressed or anything with Uncle Devin in here."

She caught Devin's smile of amusement. "Yeah, well, you know the rules. When the door is closed, you knock."

"Sorry."

"I'll get the kite out of the tree for you, Tiger," Devin said. "Go on downstairs. I'll be right there."

Jason scampered from the room.

Turning toward Lilianne, Devin let loose the chuckle he'd been holding back. "Kids," he said, shaking his head. "What time is dinner?"

"Dinner?" What did dinner have to do with kids?

"Our deal," he reminded her. "I save you from the tree and you save me from starvation."

He was a long way from starvation, she thought, taking in his solid frame. "Dinner is at six."

"Good. Set an extra place for me."

Two

When Devin came back into the house after untangling the kite from the tree, he found Lilianne in the kitchen peeling potatoes. She had showered and changed into a sundress, which he guessed she'd done for comfort's sake. He leaned against the doorjamb, content to watch her prepare dinner.

She was lovely, he thought. She had let her hair down from the constricting ponytail, and the shimmering red-gold tresses touched her shoulders in soft waves. She was also braless. His eyes zeroed in on that fact. Her breasts sloped gently beneath the cotton of her dress and swayed with each stroke of the potato peeler. The side profile he had of her enabled him to study her small nose and the full, lush lips that looked more delicious than a ripe, sweet strawberry.

Lilianne turned her head, her gaze merging with his.

Devin smiled. "Feel better?" he asked.

She returned the infectious grin. "Yes. The cream took some of the sting out."

His bold gaze traveled down her back to the vicinity of her buttocks. "Reach it okay?"

Her face turned pink. "Just fine." Picking up another potato to peel, she said, "Did you get Jason's kite out of the tree?"

"Yes."

She looked at him, her gaze softening along with her tone. "You're a hero in his eyes, you know."

The compliment warmed him, but it brought another subject to his mind. "Yeah, well, I wish *you* would stop trying to be a hero."

Puzzled, Lilianne stopped what she was doing to look at Devin. "What's that supposed to mean?"

Pushing away from the doorjamb, he came up beside her, gently brushing a wisp of hair from her cheek. "It means you shouldn't have attempted to climb that tree this afternoon."

Lilianne ignored the sensual feelings that his light touch evoked in her. Her feminine responses to him happened more and more often lately and were getting harder to control. "Jason loves that kite, Devin, you know that." She tossed the potato aside and started in on a carrot. "What was I supposed to do? Leave it in the tree?"

Smiling lazily, Devin leaned his hip against the counter beside her. "As you may recall, you weren't too successful in bringing it down."

His teasing tone didn't soften the impact of his words. Lilianne stared at him for a long moment, feeling wounded by his gentle gibe. Without replying, she resumed her task, peeling the carrot in her hand to a thin stick.

Grabbing Lilianne's arm, Devin turned her to him, forcing her full attention. "Dammit, Lily, you could have really hurt yourself!"

"I'm fine," she insisted, shaking off his hand.

"Thanks to me. What would you have done if I hadn't come along?" He gave a small chuckle, but there was little humor in it. "Hell, I bet you'd still be stuck up in that tree!"

"Thanks for the vote of confidence," she murmured as she arranged the potatoes and carrots around a seasoned pot roast.

"It's true!"

She shoved the pot into the oven and set the timer. "You're beginning to sound like Michael."

Devin's jaw hardened at the comparison. "Now, what is *that* supposed to mean?" he demanded as she washed her hands.

Lilianne turned to him, wiping her hands on a dish towel. "Michael always tried to shelter me. He never let me do anything for myself. You're the same way."

Devin crossed to her and gently took her shoulders in his hands. "I'm not trying to shelter you, Lily. You can do whatever you please, and you usually do." He let his palms slide down her bare arms until his fingers met hers. In a warm grasp, he enfolded them in his hands. "I'm concerned for your safety, sweetheart, just as I'm sure Michael was."

She turned her head away from his penetrating gaze, afraid he'd see the pain in her eyes. "No, it was more than that," she said softly.

"Lily—" Devin shut his mouth as Elizabeth and Emily strolled into the kitchen. His expression instantly softened at the younger versions of Lilianne, with their sun-kissed copper hair and emerald-green eyes. But where Lilianne was petite, the girls had inherited their father's height, and were already nearly as tall as their mother. They were beautiful girls, and they held a special spot in his heart. A smile from either of them and he turned to mush.

"Uncle Devin!" they chorused in happy surprise.

Dropping his hands from Lily's, he went to the twins, hugging and kissing them both. "How are my favorite girls?" he asked fondly.

"Fine. Great," they answered at the same time.

Devin smiled down at them, clearly remembering the day they'd been born and how proud he had been, right along with Michael. Now that Michael was gone, he felt like their protector, and he did, indeed, help Lily raise them. Like

Jason, they thought of him as an uncle, and he had worn the title proudly.

Elizabeth went to the refrigerator and peered inside. "Are you staying for dinner, Uncle Devin?" she asked over her shoulder.

His eyes caught Lily's across the kitchen. A devastatingly handsome smile claimed his lips. "Yep. My reward for rescuing your mother from the big tree out front."

Emily looked at him curiously. "What was she doing in the tree?"

Lilianne shot him a warning look, but he ignored it, his grin broadening at her expense. "She got stuck while trying to get Jason's kite down."

"Oh, no!" Elizabeth groaned dramatically, pulling the tab on a Coke. "I'm so embarrassed. I hope no one at school finds out about this."

Lifting the lid on the cookie jar sitting on the counter, Emily retrieved a handful of Oreos. "No kidding. We'll never live it down."

Used to her daughter's theatrics, Lilianne plucked the cookies from Emily's hand and put them back into the jar. "You're going to spoil your appetite."

"I'm hungry," she complained.

"Then eat an apple or a banana."

Elizabeth sidled up to Devin and whispered, "Mom just doesn't want us to eat all her Oreos so they'll be there when she gets her midnight cravings."

Devin arched a brow at Lily.

"Mom, can I get a new dress for the school dance?" Emily asked in her sweetest voice.

"We'll see."

"If Emily gets a new dress, so do I," Elizabeth said, not to be outdone by her sister.

Jason raced into the kitchen with Rusty hot on his heels. Not watching where he was heading, Jason bumped into

Elizabeth, which in turn made Rusty slam into him. Elizabeth jumped back as her Coke sloshed over the rim of the can and onto the front of her Bon Jovi T-shirt.

"Hey, watch it, squirt." Elizabeth glared at Jason as she brushed spots of Coke off Jon Bon Jovi's face.

Jason made a face at his sister. "It wasn't my fault, Rusty rammed into me."

Rusty hung his head sheepishly. "I'm sorry."

Lilianne took pity on Jason's rather quiet and shy friend. "It was just as much Jason's fault."

"Was not!" Jason protested loudly.

"You weren't watching where you were going," Emily said.

Jason's chin drew up. "I was too!"

Lilianne stifled the urge to scream in frustration. "Everybody out of the kitchen until dinner is ready," she said loudly.

The room grew quiet and they all stared at her.

"Out!" she said, pointing to the door.

They filed from the kitchen, each one grumbling their own gripes. Devin remained behind, chuckling.

Lilianne shot him an annoyed glance. "What are you laughing at?"

"You." His laughter died, but his eyes sparked brightly. "I was ready to blow a referee whistle."

"I could use one." Opening the refrigerator door, Lily reached in and grabbed a can of beer, which she handed to Devin, then poured herself a glass of iced tea.

Devin leaned against the counter and pulled the tab on his can. A fine spray erupted from the puncture. He took a long swallow. "Cravings for Oreo cookies in the middle of the night, huh?"

His seductive tone touched her spine, sending chills over the surface of her nerves. "So I like Oreo cookies," she said defensively.

Devin's smile was slow in coming, tempting her with a hint of devilry. He leaned toward her, his eyes falling to her mouth. "Tell me, Lily, do you like to eat the whole cookie or are you one of those people who nibbles the cream center off first?"

Unconsciously Lilianne ran her tongue over her bottom lip. "I like to nibble the . . ." She shook her head, snapping herself out of her hypnotic daze. She frowned. "What does it matter how I like to eat my cookies?"

Shrugging, he took a drink of beer. "How a person eats an Oreo tells you how sensual they are."

She rolled her eyes. "You're joking."

"No, I'm not." He looked totally serious until his mouth spilled into a wicked grin. "I'd be willing to bet you're a real sensual cookie eater."

"Can we please drop the subject of cookies?" Who would have thought discussing Oreos could be so arousing? Face flaming, she turned toward the sink and began rinsing dishes.

Devin chuckled. He swallowed the rest of his beer, then crushed the can in his hand. He came up beside Lilianne, pressing the back of his hand against her hip.

Lilianne's eyes flew to his as a slow, burning heat seared her through her dress.

"I need to throw this way," he said, showing her the reason he'd been trying to nudge her over.

Lilianne stared at the crushed can in Devin's hand. "Oh." She stepped to the side, allowing him room to open the cupboard beneath the sink. He dropped the beer can into the plastic bin for aluminum cans.

"I told Jason I'd toss a football with him and Rusty before dinner," Devin said. "We'll be washed up and ready to eat by six."

"Fine. I've got some things to finish up in the office." She watched him leave, wondering at the fluttering sensation in her stomach.

Lilianne sat in the small office in the back of the house, which was once filled with Michael's legal books, papers and degrees. She had since redecorated the room to reflect the business workings of her interior-design company. Books carrying swatches of material and assorted scraps of wallpaper were lined up on the bookcase she'd had installed. Awards for her interior designs done on model homes hung on the wall, testimony to how hard she'd worked over the past two years. The carpet was a soft cream color, the wallpaper a floral pattern of mauve and blue. The window was framed in a valance, cut short with a ruffled edge.

Lilianne tried concentrating on the order of draperies, blinds and wallpaper laid out on the polished desk before her, but her mind refused to cooperate. All she could think about was Devin who, with his tight jeans and sexy smile, set her heart to racing.

Propping her chin in her hands, she tried deciphering the odd mixture of feelings stirring inside her. She'd always cared for Devin, she reasoned, ever since Michael had first introduced him to her. Lately, though, her feelings were growing into something more than simple friendship. Her reaction to his touch put her feminine senses on alert.

Devin had been Michael's best friend for so long Lilianne couldn't remember a time when Devin hadn't been a part of the family. When Michael died, Devin had been there for her, the twins and Jason, helping them through that difficult time.

Remorse rushed through her. Compounded with the pain of losing Michael was the guilt she felt over the sequence of events that had snowballed the months before his death.

Lilianne could vividly remember the arguments she and Michael had had about his spending so much time at the office and so little time with her and the kids. The conflict and tension between them became unbearable, and pretty soon they were virtual strangers living under the same roof.

Then Jason started school, and she was alone during the day, with nothing to fill those long hours. She wanted to go back to work, but the suggestion had been met with staunch opposition from Michael. He'd always controlled the direction of her life, never allowed her any independence. He refused to let her go back to work.

The arguments became more frequent.

Then came the ultimatum, followed by the car accident that had claimed Michael's life.

And now, three years later, she was beginning to feel things for Michael's best friend that confused her. When Devin touched her she felt a strange melting sensation in the pit of her stomach. Her response to him was increasing in frequency, causing her emotions to tumble.

"How's business?"

Lilianne visibly jumped. She looked up to see Devin standing in the doorway. He leaned negligently against the frame, arms crossed over his chest. His shirt, damp with sweat from playing ball with the boys, was molded to his torso. His thick hair was tousled and his eyes sparkled with mischief.

Pushing away from the door, Devin entered the room. "Sorry, didn't mean to startle you."

Lilianne began stacking the papers on her desk. "It's okay. I was engrossed in the order I need to place for the Hartford Model homes." She stood, knowing she'd be working late into the night writing up the purchase order. It wouldn't be the first time her thoughts had wandered to the man now in her doorway and her work had gone neglected. "I need to set the table for dinner, anyway."

"I'll help." He followed her out of the office to the kitchen.

Lilianne opened the cupboard above the counter and stood on tiptoe, reaching for the dinner plates on the second shelf.

Devin reached above her and grabbed the plates for her. As he did so, he crowded her into the counter, the front of his body rubbing against her back. "I'll set the table," he offered.

With conscious effort, Lilianne regulated her breathing. His touch had sent flames licking up her spine. Lately, whenever she came into contact with him, the effect was like spontaneous combustion. If only he knew what he did to her senses.

"So how's business?" he asked again, ambling to the oak table set up in the next room. He placed a plate in front of each chair.

Lilianne stepped to the refrigerator and pulled out a fruit salad she had prepared earlier. She closed the door with her hip. "Great. I should be starting the Hartford model homes next week."

He looked up, seeing her above the half wall separating the kitchen from the dining room. "That's a pretty big account, isn't it?"

Lilianne smiled as she put the bowl in the middle of the table. "For me it is. I'm almost finished with the Meadowbrook Development Project. Will you go to the grand opening with me?"

"You bet. I wouldn't miss it." Opening the silverware drawer, Devin pulled out five knives and forks. "Quite the businesswoman, aren't you?" he teased.

"Thanks to you," she said sincerely. She couldn't thank him enough. He had urged her to follow her dream and launch her own business with part of Michael's insurance money. He had been her main support the whole time.

He shrugged off her appreciation. "No thanks needed. You're the one with the eye for color and design, not me." He placed a knife and fork at each setting. "I barely know the difference between polka dots and stripes."

She laughed, grabbing a few pot holders from a drawer. Turning on the light in the oven, she peered through the window, satisfied that the pot roast had browned nicely. Opening the door, she tested the vegetables with a fork. Assured that the meal was done, she picked up the pot holders she'd left on the counter. Just as she bent over to retrieve the roast, Devin came up behind her and snatched the pot holders from her hands.

"Here, let me do that," he said, gently nudging her aside.

Lilianne's mouth opened to refuse his offer, but he already had the roast in his hands and was strolling to the table with it.

Lilianne called the kids to dinner. The girls talked about the school dance coming up, and Jason went on about a camping trip planned for a group of his friends at the end of the month. All three vied for Devin's attention. Unable to get a word in edgewise, Lilianne sat back, enjoying the lively conversation. Every so often Devin would look up at her and give her one of his special winks and a smile.

At a lull in the conversation, Lilianne jumped in while she had the chance. "I received a call from school today," she said casually, noting how all three kids stopped eating to stare at her with nervous expressions.

"Uh, whose school?" Elizabeth asked tentatively.

"Yours."

Jason resumed shoveling carrots into his mouth while Elizabeth's and Emily's eyes widened.

"What did they want?" Emily asked. "I swear we haven't done anything wrong." She cast a glance at her sister. "At least *I* haven't."

Elizabeth glared at her sister. "I've been good." Smiling like an angel with a crooked halo, she switched her gaze to Lilianne. "Well, what did they want?"

Lilianne took a sip of iced tea, then wiped her mouth with her napkin, deliberately taking her time.

"Mother!" the twins said in unison.

She had to smile. "Mrs. Bailey called to ask me if I'd chaperon the school dance. They're short two volunteers."

"What did you tell her?" Elizabeth demanded.

"I told her yes, of course." Lilianne cut a slice of roast. "I don't have plans for that weekend, and Jason will be camping with his friends."

"You can't be a chaperon," Elizabeth said, horror in her voice.

"This is worse than enduring Mr. Horner's frogs in science class," Emily groaned, covering her face with her hands.

"A fate worse than death?" Devin supplied, amusement pulling at his lips.

"Nothing is worse than having your parent be a chaperon at a dance," Elizabeth informed Devin. Then she looked at her mom. "No offense, Mom, but it just isn't cool."

Devin chuckled.

Reaching across the table, Lilianne patted Elizabeth's hand consolingly. "No offense taken, honey. But since I'm on the PTA, Mrs. Bailey reminded me that I haven't chaperoned yet this year."

"Why couldn't you have told her you'd be sick or something that weekend?" Elizabeth said, pouting.

Tipping back his chair, Devin's chuckle turned to all-out laughter.

Lilianne lifted a brow at him. "Find this amusing, do you, Devin?"

He clutched his stomach. "Very."

"Well, that's nice, because I volunteered you for the other chaperon."

His laughter ceased. The two front legs of his chair hit the floor with a jarring thud. "You did what?"

"Radical!" Emily said.

"Cool!" Elizabeth added.

Jason ignored them all and helped himself to a second serving of fruit salad.

Lilianne flashed Devin a cunning smile. She hadn't really volunteered him for the other chaperon, but his amusement at her expense had annoyed her. She'd call Mrs. Bailey and remedy the situation. Lilianne was sure Mrs. Bailey wouldn't mind having an extra chaperon.

"Lilianne," Devin said, his expression serious. "I can't chaperon a school dance."

"Sure you can. It's quite simple. No parental skills required." She buttered the corner of her roll and took a bite, hiding her smile.

"Please say you'll go, Uncle Devin," Elizabeth pleaded, giving him her best doe-eyed look.

"It'll be so cool if you go with Mom, please?" Emily added. "No boy is going to ask us to dance if Mom is hanging around. If you go, you can keep her busy." She grinned up at Devin, obviously pleased with her reasoning.

The look Devin shot Lilianne clearly stated he'd get even with her. Then a wicked gleam entered his eyes. Leaning forward, he rested his elbows on the table. "Keep your mom busy, huh? Now that's kind of appealing."

Had his voice turned low and husky, or had she only imagined it had? She met his steady gaze, saw the sexy, uninhibited curve of his lips, and her insides began to unravel and melt.

"It'll be so *cool* if you go with Mom." Emily gazed up at Devin with adoration.

"I'll go," he said slowly and deliberately, "as long as your mother promises me a dance."

Lilianne's fork stopped in midair. The thought of her body flush against his sent her hormones in a frenzy. Of course, he hadn't specified a slow dance. She looked up at him. "It's a deal."

It was Emily's turn to do the dishes, Elizabeth's to clear the table and Jason's to empty the trash. They went about their chores without complaint while Lilianne and Devin went outside to the backyard.

Devin watched Lilianne fill a plastic container with water and start watering the plants hanging from the patio beams. He sat down in a glider chair and laced his fingers over his stomach. The sun was retiring for the evening, spreading glorious streaks of purple, orange and red across the Colorado sky.

"Did you get an invitation to Amy and Richard's wedding?" Lilianne asked. Her back faced Devin as she tended to a creeping Charlie.

The engaged couple were mutual friends of theirs. "Yes." Devin stretched out his long legs and reclined in the chair, feeling full and lazy after her delicious meal. He could get used to this, he thought.

She looked over her shoulder at him. "Are you going with anyone?" she asked.

Devin had had his share of women, but he never dated anyone long enough to get serious. His relationships usually fizzled out before the commitment stage, which suited him just fine. He liked female companionship, but there was only one lifetime mate he wanted, and she treated him like a brother. He sighed.

"Haven't really thought about a date," he answered. He hadn't even sent back the RSVP card yet. "How about you?"

"No date." She picked a dead flower off her fuchsia plant and tossed it into the small bucket beside her. "I'm going solo."

He should have known. His eyes slid down her back, immediately picking up on the fact that she wasn't wearing a slip. The dying sun silhouetted her long legs and outlined her hips. "Why don't you date, Lily?" he asked without thinking.

She turned around to face him. "I date," she said, a curious expression on her face.

He thought about these so-called dates. One had been a banker who had been as stuffy as the starched shirt and tie he'd been wearing. Another had been a teacher at a nearby college, whose conversations droned on like lectures and bored her to death, Lilianne had told him. "You've dated some real winners, Lily," he said sardonically. "You've only dated about four times in the three years that Michael's been gone. And I know you've even refused a couple at that."

She bent to refill her container. "I don't want to get tied down," she answered. That was true. She didn't ever want to live under someone's thumb again.

"I'm not talking about marriage, Lily," he said. "I'm talking about male companionship. You're a desirable woman with a woman's needs."

"Leave it to you, Mr. McKay, to be blunt and straight-forward," she said with a wry grin.

He sat up, resting his elbows on his knees. "It's the truth. And I know plenty of men who'd love to ask you out, but you refuse more than you accept. You're very attractive and sexy."

"I'd hardly call stretch marks on my stomach sexy," she said.

"You have terrific legs and a nice, uh, backside." He grinned wolfishly. "Take it from me. I saw part of it earlier."

Her face turned pink. "You didn't see anything."

"I saw enough."

She shook her head at him. "What's the big deal about me dating, anyway? I've got a career and family to worry about."

Yeah, he thought, what was the big deal? Did he really want to see her date and get serious with someone when he wanted her for himself? What he really wanted was for her to date him. Did he even have a chance when she considered him nothing more than a friend?

"I didn't mean to nag you," he said, connecting with her green eyes. "Since neither one of us has a date for the wedding, why don't we go together?"

She removed a weed from the planter running alongside the house. "That would be fine."

He smiled, pleased. "Great. The wedding is at five, so I'll pick you up around four."

She looked up, a soft smile curving her mouth. "It's a date."

He only wished it were.

Three

Although the wedding wasn't officially a date, it felt like one. Lilianne took the opportunity to wear her best dress and purchase a new bottle of exotic, expensive perfume. Applying her cosmetics with a steady hand, she took extra pains to highlight her green eyes. She had her hair styled and curled, and it fell in soft red-gold waves to her shoulders. By the time she finished, she felt like a million bucks.

Her dress, a teal-colored silk, slithered over her body to her knees. A matching sash wrapped around her hips, bisecting the dress into two tantalizing pieces. The neckline cut into a V to her breasts, showing a modest amount of cleavage. She completed the outfit with high-heeled black pumps.

Lilianne heard Devin's Bronco pull into the drive. After checking her appearance in the mirror one last time, she grabbed her clutch purse and headed to the living room. Emily had just let Devin in.

"Wow!" Jason said in surprise. "You look great, Mom."

"Thank you, sweetie," she said, bending down to drop a quick kiss on his head. His honest praise warmed her. She looked up, meeting Devin's appreciative gaze. Smiling softly, she waited for his reaction.

"You do look nice, Lily," Devin said evenly.

"Thanks." Lilianne's bubble burst. That wasn't exactly the response she had anticipated. Maybe she had dressed too conservatively for his taste. "You look nice, too." Lilianne admired the three-piece pin-striped suit that fit his frame to perfection. The suit jacket clung to his wide shoulders, tapering to his lean hips. He looked resplendent, very different from his usual rough-and-ready appearance. His hair had been artfully blow-dried, his face freshly shaven. Citrusy after-shave curled around her senses, smelling clean and crisp.

"You look very handsome, Uncle Devin," Elizabeth said shyly.

"Thank you." Devin gave Elizabeth one of his heart-stopping grins. Slipping his hand into his trouser pocket, he jingled his keys and turned to Lily. "Ready to go?"

She nodded, then addressed the kids. "Take care of your brother, girls. Mrs. Collins next door knows you're here by yourselves, so if you need anything you can call her."

"We'll be fine, Mom," Emily said.

Lilianne smoothed back Emily's silky hair, smiling gently. "I know. I worry too much." The few times she had gone out, she had left Jason in the twins' care, and they'd taken their responsibility seriously.

Devin and Lilianne had decided to go in her white volvo, and he ushered her toward it now, his hand at her waist. He could feel the subtle, sexy sway of her hips. He opened the passenger-side door and waited for her to slide in. As she did, her dress rode up to her thighs, giving him a brief glimpse of sheer stockinged leg before she pulled the silk back down. Desire thrummed through his veins. Damn! She had his body responding to hers like a schoolboy's.

As Devin backed the Volvo down the driveway past his Bronco, he said, "I'm still trying to find the spare time to paint that thing." He figured he'd try for a neutral conversation to keep things on an even keel. "I've been so busy at the body shop with repairs and restorations I don't have the time or room to paint it."

Lilianne glanced over at the primered Bronco. "Oh, I don't know. I think that dull, flat gray color is very becoming."

He chuckled. "Yeah, I'm kind of getting used to it myself. I'd hate to spoil the effect with a smooth glossy coating of black paint."

"So business is good?" she asked, looking over at him.

He nodded. "I've had to hire two more guys to do the bodywork. Pretty soon I'm going to have to find a bigger garage to accommodate all the work."

Devin smiled, remembering the five years he'd spent struggling since first opening his body shop. Slowly but surely business was prospering. He was finally making a name for himself. Word of mouth traveled fast. That and the fact he did beautiful, impeccable work, guaranteeing all bodywork and paint jobs. He rarely had a dissatisfied customer.

Devin turned onto the freeway, picking up speed. "I've got more backup work than I can handle. Cars that need bodywork, company trucks that need new logos on them, people with boats who want them painted and sealed. Just today I received a call from the school district. They want me to strip and repaint their school buses." The pride in his voice was unmistakable.

Devin went on about his body shop, appropriately named McKay's Body Works, but Lilianne wasn't paying any attention. Her gaze was riveted to his profile. She studied his brows, his chiseled cheekbones and square, strong jaw. His nose had a slight bump in it, caused when she, Devin and Michael had gone hiking in the mountains while they were in high school. Not paying attention to where he was going, Devin had walked into a low tree branch and broken his nose. The permanent bump was a souvenir of that lazy spring day.

The memories of the three of them together made Lily smile. They'd forged a special bond that had lasted through the years. Now it was just her and Devin. She couldn't help but wonder if somehow she was being unfaithful to Michael's memory for her growing attraction to his best friend.

Pushing the confusing thought aside, she continued to study Devin's profile. Her gaze fell to his lips, opening and closing in a steady stream of words. They were nice lips, full and sensual. Those lips had kissed her cheek many times in a brotherly sort of way. She wondered what they'd feel like moving over her lips, her neck, her breasts. A tiny moan escaped her throat.

"Are you okay?" Devin asked, staring at her intently.

Lilianne's face heated and she looked away, mortified that such a thought would enter her mind at a time like this. "I . . . I'm fine," she said.

"You were looking at me strangely," he said.

"I was just thinking." She kept her face averted, staring out the window until she felt the blush fade. She wished it was dark out, but it was only four-thirty.

"About what?" Draping his wrist over the steering wheel, Devin placed his other hand on the middle console. He glanced over at her.

I was thinking about your incredible lips on mine. "Uhh . . . nothing," she said lamely.

"You were thinking about nothing?" he persisted, a hint of a smile curling his lips.

"Yes," she said indignantly, green eyes flashing. "I was thinking of nothing."

He chuckled, infuriating her further. "You're blushing, Lily." His tone dropped, low and intimate, as if privy to her innermost thoughts.

She fanned herself with her hand. "It's warm in the car," she grumbled as an excuse, even as the Volvo's air conditioner blasted her with near-freezing air.

"Sure." Devin graciously let the subject drop.

The wedding ceremony was simple and gracious. By the time they got to the reception, which was being held at a country club a few miles away from the church, darkness had fallen. Inside the banquet room the tables were draped in white linen, and chandeliers sparkled from above. A band tuned up their instruments as the guests milled around, waiting for the bride and groom to arrive.

Lily knew most of the same people Devin did. They were standing in a circle of friends when a male voice sounded from behind her.

"Hey, McKay!"

They both turned. A sandy-haired man approached, and Devin stuck out his hand. "Hi, Steve. How's the paint job holding up?"

"Beautifully."

Lilianne studied Steve. He wasn't anyone she knew. Polished and classically handsome, he looked like a business executive. The fingers wrapped around the champagne glass he held were perfectly manicured.

"Steve, this a friend of mine, Lilianne Austin," Devin said politely. "Lilianne, this is Steve Hayes. He's a customer of mine. I've painted his Corvette and I just got through painting his speedboat."

Lilianne didn't miss the way the man's eyes slid over her in open appraisal. "It's nice to meet you, Mr. Hayes."

He laughed. "Call me Steve." He looked back at Devin. "A friend, you say?"

Devin hesitated for a brief second. He wished he had the right to claim her as more. To confirm her as a friend put her on the open market for Steve to pursue. And Devin had no doubt Steve would. The other man had a gleam in his eyes that implied definite male interest. Devin gritted his teeth and forced the words out of his mouth. "Yes. Lilianne and I have been friends for years."

Devin's irritation increased when Steve joined them at their table for dinner. Lilianne sat between the two, her attention constantly diverted by Steve, who poured on the charm, flattering her with compliments, until Devin thought he was going to lose his meal.

Devin swallowed a bite of his chicken with wine-and-mushroom sauce, seething at Steve's cool, suave manners. Mrs. Weatherbee, an elderly grandmotherly woman, sat next to Devin, talking about how her cat was always choking on fur balls. Devin couldn't ignore her, so he listened to her inane chitchat while trying to keep an ear on Lilianne and Steve's conversation. He smothered the anger that threatened to explode and tried replacing it with a calm he didn't feel. He hadn't planned on sharing Lilianne tonight. Especially with a womanizer like Steve!

The band began playing, and Devin took the opportunity to excuse himself from Mrs. Weatherbee and ask Lilianne to dance. He wasn't taking no for an answer.

"Save a dance for me," Steve said as Lilianne walked away with Devin.

Lilianne looked over her shoulder, smiling sweetly in answer.

"Not likely, chump," Devin muttered under his breath.

They danced two fast songs and when a slow song began to play, Devin didn't hesitate to gather Lilianne in his arms. He didn't ask her if she wanted to dance to the slow tune. He didn't give her a chance.

Devin gazed into Lilianne's flushed face, enjoying the way her green eyes sparkled. Her hair, which tumbled in artful disarray around her face, made his fingers itch to slide through the tresses, feel their silky softness. Pulling her closer, he felt sparks of desire course through his body. The feel of her lush curves, her soft breasts pressed to his hard chest, made his heart pound wildly. Daringly, Devin's hand roamed down her back and paused just above her buttocks, rubbing, pressing the sensitive hollow of her spine.

The exotic smell of Lilianne's perfume intoxicated Devin. It wrapped around him, causing his blood to thicken. Catching her heavy-lidded gaze, he held it, then slowly lowered his eyes to her lips. He nearly groaned when her tongue darted out and moistened her bottom lip. Tracking his way back to her eyes, he silently pleaded for permission to taste the sweetness of her mouth.

Lips parting on a breathy sigh, she gave it to him.

"You are so beautiful," he whispered, his head lowering in slow increments.

The sensual bubble cocooning them popped when Steve cut in. He did it so quickly and so skillfully Devin didn't get a chance to protest. Before Devin could comprehend what had happened, Lilianne was out of his arms and in Steve's. Devin stood there, dumbfounded, as Steve whirled Lilianne away. Steve grinned triumphantly over Lilianne's shoulder at Devin.

Fuming, Devin went to the bar and ordered a drink. He watched Steve say something to Lilianne, and Lilianne tilt her head back and laugh. He curbed the urge to punch Steve in his handsome face. He also restrained himself from marching over and snatching Steve's hand away from the curve of Lilianne's hip. How could she let him manhandle her like that? A wave of jealousy gripped his insides in an iron fist. He tossed back a shot of whiskey, wincing as it burned a path to his stomach.

Lilianne forced a smile for Steve, tamping down the warm feelings still swirling inside her from Devin's touch. Why had Devin given her up so easily to Steve? For a moment she thought she had captivated him, that he'd been about to kiss her. She had obviously mistaken the admiration in his eyes for real desire. She shook her head, feeling like a fool for entertaining the notion that there was more to their relationship than friendship. Sighing, she turned her attention to her new dance partner, who was holding her annoyingly close.

"Would you like to go out sometime?" Steve asked her just as she reined in her thoughts of Devin.

She smiled at him, trying to find an easy way to let him down. "I don't have much time to date," she said kindly. "My business and children keep me far too busy."

"Surely you can take time out to have a little fun?" His eyes sparkled devilishly at the word fun.

"I really don't have time." Searching the banquet room, Lilianne found Devin brooding over at the bar. She wondered what had put him in such a sour mood. She watched as an attractive brunette approached him. They talked for a few minutes, then Devin's eyes found Lilianne's. Grasping the brunette's elbow, he led her to the dance floor, pulling her close.

Lilianne's back stiffened as Devin charmed the woman into peals of laughter.

"Is there something going on between you and Devin?" Steve asked, following her gaze.

Lilianne's head snapped back to Steve. "Of course not." She didn't know if she was trying to convince him or herself.

"They why not go out with me?"

Yeah, why not? After all, it wasn't as though Devin was pining for her. Just last week he had urged her to date. But even though Steve was a good-looking guy with a witty sense of humor, she couldn't envision dating him. "I'm sorry. Now isn't a very good time for me."

Steve gave her a light squeeze. "Fine. I understand. Maybe some other time."

Lilianne remained in Steve's company for the remainder of the evening. His persistence left her with little choice. She saw Devin often, always with the brunette. A streak of pain lanced through her when Devin bent his head to speak intimately with the woman and she twined her hands through the hair at the back of his neck. Lilianne didn't fully understand her reaction, especially since she'd never felt such jealousy before. She had to keep reminding herself that Devin was just a friend, a big brother in a sense, nothing more.

Devin finally approached her around midnight. He swaggered up to the table where she sat talking to Steve, and his expression was thunderous. "Are you ready to go, Lily?" he asked in an icy tone.

What had she done to earn his contempt? she wondered. He had been the one who had given her up so freely to Steve to spend his evening with a racy brunette who couldn't control her wandering hands. If Steve's presence bothered him it was his own damn fault.

Lilianne stood up and Steve followed suit. "Steve has offered to take me home," she said.

Devin's mood turned blacker. "If you've forgotten, we drove your car."

"You have to drive it to my place to pick up your Bronco, anyway," she said reasonably.

"Lily..." There was no way Devin was going to let that octopus be alone with her. He didn't want him putting the moves on an innocent widow like Lily.

Grabbing her arm, he excused her from Steve's presence. When they were out of earshot, Devin started in on her. "That's incredibly rude, you know." He pushed back his jacket and placed his hands on his hips. "You came to this wedding with me and I expect you to leave with me."

Lilianne couldn't help noticing how sexy he looked. His hair was attractively tousled from being finger-combed by the brunette, and his eyes, a dark, sensual brown fringed with thick lashes, sparked with anger. His stance, arrogant, cocky and possessive, thrilled her.

"You're right," she conceded. "That was rude of me. I'm sorry."

Devin frowned. He had expected an argument, not this easy submission. Damn it, he *wanted* an argument to blow off some of this steam!

"I'll just tell Steve good-night and then I'll be ready to go."

Devin watched her walk back to Steve, aggravation and frustration curling his toes. When Steve smiled at her and ran his hand intimately down her arm, he thought he'd explode. He spun around and strode to the door before the wedding reception turned into a brawl.

Devin remained quiet and withdrawn as they started toward home, still smoldering over Lily's apparent interest in Steve. At least he'd been successful in getting her to go home with him, rather than have her accept a ride in the close confines of Steve's Corvette. No telling how Steve might have taken advantage of her.

Drawing a deep breath, Devin rolled his shoulders, trying to release the tension coiling his body as tight as a spring. He kept his eyes trained on the road, hating the awkward silence stretching between them.

"Are you upset with me?" Lilianne asked softly when they turned into her street. She tilted her head, her hair spilling over her shoulder in a riot of curls.

Devin knew he had no valid reason to be. He relaxed his clenched jaw. Glancing her way, he saw her worried expression and offered her a halfhearted smile. "No."

"Then what's wrong?" she asked. "You've been acting weird all evening."

"Yeah, I know. I'm sorry." What excuse could he give? He couldn't very well tell her he was as jealous as hell and didn't want any man other than himself around her, let alone touching her, especially after giving her a lecture on dating the week before. "I've been under a lot of stress at the shop lately," he lied. Feeling like a jerk for treating her so badly, he wanted to make amends. "So what's new with Steve?" he asked conversationally, forcing his tone to be light.

"He asked me out on a date," she said nonchalantly.

Devin's blood turned to ice in his veins. "Lily, are you crazy?" His fingers clutched the steering wheel. He pulled the Volvo into her driveway and brought it to an abrupt halt. He jammed the car into park and turned toward her, his expression grim.

Crossing her arms over her chest, Lilianne met Devin's burning stare. "You don't like him very much, do you?" she asked tightly, wondering if Devin was jealous.

"I like him as a customer and acquaintance just fine," he stated brusquely. Turning off the engine, he handed her the key, nearly imprinting it in her palm. "But I don't want you to go out with him."

Even though she had no intention of dating Steve, Lilianne bristled. "I don't think I need your permission to go out with Steve."

He tried to remain calm. "Lily, he's not your type."

Ah, now she understood. Devin was playing big brother, trying to protect his little sister's virtue. It was the last thing she wanted from him. "What do you know about my type?"

"Steve Hayes is a womanizer. You'll end up getting hurt, Lily. The man has more moves than a football player. He uses women."

Cocking a brow, Lilianne smiled ever so slightly. "Need I remind you it was your idea for me to start dating again?"

Steve Hayes had not been what he'd had in mind. "No, you don't need to remind me," he mimicked. "But why in hell couldn't you pick someone who treats women with respect?"

She smiled. Maybe he really *was* jealous! "You're jealous," she said.

"I am not," he grumbled. "I'm just concerned about who you date."

Opening the car door, she looked over at him. The interior light made the crease of concern between his brows more prominent. She'd made him suffer long enough, she thought. "Concern yourself no more. I told him no." She slipped out of the car, closing the door on his astonished expression.

Devin watched Lilianne walk around the front of the car, his fingers itching to wrap around her neck. She'd put him through hell! Getting out of the car, he escorted her to the front porch, his temper cooling on the short walk. He took the key from her hand and opened the door.

Lilianne pivoted toward Devin, smiling. The porch light cast a halo around her red-gold hair, making her look bewitching. Her eyes glimmered like green pools. "Thanks for going to the wedding with me, Devin. It was better than going alone." Placing her hand on his chest, she stood on tip toe to give him a chaste kiss on the cheek.

At the last second Devin turned his head and her lips landed on his mouth. Devin didn't want the sort of good-night kiss they usually shared. Her lips lingered on his a few seconds, as if savoring the feel of him, the taste, then she abruptly pulled away.

Lilianne retreated a step, shocked by the spark of desire the simple kiss had set off in her. Her lips tingled and her stomach fluttered. Had he moved his head intentionally? The innocent look in his eyes confused her.

"Good night, Lily," Devin said, as if nothing out of the ordinary had happened, though she couldn't help note the husky timbre of his voice.

"Good night, Devin." Closing the door behind her, she leaned against it for support, legs quaking. She wondered if she had imagined the intensity of the kiss. She wondered if Devin's heart was beating as erratically as hers.

Devin got into his Bronco and gunned the engine, grinning for the first time since the wedding. The kiss had rattled her. He also knew if he had chosen to pursue the kiss she would have let him. Knowing that was enough to send his spirits soaring.

Four

Devin could smell the sweet fragrance of chocolate the moment he removed his helmet. After hooking it on the back of his motorcycle, he followed the aroma all the way to Lily's front door.

"It's me," he called, opening the screen door and letting himself in.

"I'm in the kitchen, Devin," Lilianne said.

He strolled into the kitchen, instantly assaulted by the delicious baking odors. A couple of dozen cupcakes, sitting on cooling racks, lined the counter in a neat row. A big bowl of frosting sat next to them, a spatula sticking out of the gooey concoction. The sink, piled high with dirty dishes coated in flour and chocolate, attested to all the work.

Swiping one of the warm cupcakes off the rack, he peeled back the paper wrapper and sunk his teeth into it. The cupcake tasted moist and rich, satisfying his grumbling stomach.

"Hey," Lilianne said, wiping her cheek with the back of her hand, leaving behind a streak of chocolate. "Those aren't for you to eat."

He swallowed his mouthful of cupcake, raising his brows in mock surprise. "No?"

She scooped chocolate batter into a paper cupcake liner. "No. They're for the PTA bake sale at Jason's school. I've been working all morning trying to get them done."

"You look like it."

She wrinkled her nose at him. "Gee, thanks. I know I look a wreck, but I wasn't exactly expecting company. Seeing as you drop by anytime you feel like it, you'll have to suffer with a less than perfect me."

He'd suffer those consequences anytime, he thought. She looked just as tempting as her cupcakes. Her hair had been pulled back into a ponytail, leaving red-gold wisps framing her face. Since the oven had been on, the kitchen was warm, and she had on a halter top to keep her cool, leaving her smooth back naked and exposed. The creamy expanse of skin tempted the tips of his fingers.

Finishing his cupcake, Devin let his gaze wander over her white shorts and down her shapely legs to her pink-painted toenails. Oh yeah, he'd suffer seeing her like this anytime.

Lilianne turned toward Devin, giving him the full impact of her curvaceous body. "So, what do you think?"

Devin jerked his gaze to hers, the last of the cupcake catching in his throat like a sticky web. "Of what?" he asked.

She sighed impatiently, as if dealing with a small child. "The cupcakes. What else?"

She'd be shocked to her toes if she really knew what else. He cleared his throat. "It was great."

She cast a tired look at the cooling cupcakes. "I still have to frost them." She glanced at the clock over the sink. "Carolyn's coming to pick them up in less than two hours. I'll never get them done in time."

The timer on the oven went off, indicating the next batch of cupcakes was ready. Lilianne pulled them out.

"Can I help?" he asked, watching her scurry around the kitchen.

Lilianne looked over her shoulder at him, weighing the sincerity of his offer. What man liked to spend his spare time in the kitchen? Holding one end of the hot cupcake tin with a pot holder, she flipped the tin to dump out the cupcakes. The hot pan hit her hand, singeing the inside of her wrist. She immediately dropped it. "Damn!"

A red, angry blister immediately surfaced. Her eyes watered from the pain. Looking up, she found Devin beside her, reaching for her hand.

"Let me see," he said, turning her arm over to inspect the burn.

She sucked in a breath. His touch singed worse than the metal had. "I'm okay."

Pulling her to the sink, he turned on the tap, then thrust her wrist beneath the cold flow. He held her arm, making sure she didn't move.

"Devin, it's not that bad. I'm fine." The feel of the cool water sluicing over her wrist and Devin's thumb stroking the pulse point just below the burn had a slow heat simmering in the pit of her belly. She wanted to jerk her hand from him, but knew how foolish she'd look if she did.

"Do you have first-aid spray for burns?" Stopping the water, Devin examined the blister, then turned on the water once more.

"It's in the medicine cabinet in the bathroom." She looked up at him, trying to regulate her breathing when his gaze dropped to her mouth. "I'm fine, Devin. Really."

He let go of her arm, ignoring her words. "Don't move. I'll be right back."

Lilianne drew a deep breath when Devin disappeared from the kitchen. What in the world was wrong with her? His touch nearly made her knees give way. Looking over at the cupcakes cluttering the counter, she groaned. She'd never have them all frosted and ready to go in time.

"You okay?" Devin asked, returning from his errand, his brow etched in concern.

She realized he'd heard her groan. "I'm fine. I'm just thinking about all these cupcakes I have to frost."

"I'll help you." Shutting off the water, Devin dabbed the moisture from the burn with the kitchen towel. He aimed the first-aid spray and fired. A fine mist settled over the blister. "There, that should help take away the sting." He grinned at her. "Hey, is this the same stuff you used on your fanny?"

Grinning back, she said, "No, I used an ointment." She grew serious. "You really don't have to, you know."

He placed a gauze bandage over the blister and ran a piece of surgical tape over it to hold it in place. "Don't have to what?"

"Help me with the cupcakes." Lilianne shifted on her feet, wishing his fingers weren't everywhere, touching her arm, her wrist, her palm, her fingers.

"I want to," he said. "I love making cupcakes."

She'd bet he'd never made a cupcake in his life. Her suspicions were confirmed after he attempted to frost the first one. A blob of chocolate frosting, two inches high, sat on top of his cupcake. He'd gotten half that much on the paper liner, making it impossible to pick up the cupcake without getting her fingers sticky with frosting.

Lilianne plucked the next cupcake from his fingers. "Here, I'll frost them. You put the sprinkles on them." She handed him a plastic shaker filled with colorful, edible confetti.

Smearing frosting on her cupcake, she quickly finished it, handing it over to Devin in a two-man assembly line. She stopped briefly only to take the last tray of cupcakes out of the oven.

FREE ISSUE

plus a *FREE GIFT*

FREE Romance Magazine!

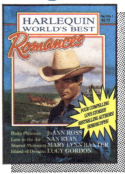

Finally—the perfect romance magazine for today's busy woman! *World's Best Romances* fits easily in pocket or purse, and each issue features *four complete romance stories* by the world's bestselling romance authors.

These are short, passionate love stories, perfect for those occasions when you don't have a lot of time! Send for your free issue today and you'll also get a beautiful gold-tone necklace just for giving us a try!

World's Best Romances is not available in stores, but you can send for a copy with no obligation to subscribe! When your free issue arrives, read one of these wonderful stories and you'll be hooked! If you like our magazine and wish to continue, you'll get 5 more bimonthly issues (making 6 in all) for just $10.96—that's a 33% savings off the cover price, and quite a bargain! Or write "cancel" on the invoice we'll send, return it and owe nothing. No matter what you decide, the free issue and necklace are yours to keep. Either way you can't lose, and we think you'll be glad you gave us a try!

J93001001

NAME

ADDRESS   APT.

CITY   STATE   ZIP

© 1993 HARLEQUIN ENTERPRISES LTD   **Printed in the U.S.A.**

A beautiful free gift for you!

This beautiful gold-tone necklace will add an elegant touch to any outfit! It's yours absolutely free when you accept your free issue of *World's Best Romances!* Hurry—return the postage-paid card right away!

20" in length, jewel clasp

"Michael hardly ever stepped into the kitchen, let alone offered to help," Lilianne said as she passed Devin another cupcake, then licked a speck of frosting off her thumb.

"I'm not Michael," Devin said, a bit of irritation in his voice.

"Yeah, well, most men believe a woman's place is in the kitchen. You know, barefoot and pregnant."

Looking over at Lilianne, Devin wiggled his eyebrows at her. "I agree with the pregnant part. Especially what comes beforehand."

She shot him a sharp look.

Devin placed a confettied cupcake in a box Lilianne had put out for finished cupcakes. "There's nothing wrong with a man wanting his wife to be pregnant. I think it's kind of sexy."

Frowning, she scooped out a knifeful of frosting from the bowl. "Michael would have kept me permanently pregnant if I'd let him."

Devin's look turned lecherous. "A randy old fellow, eh?"

She shook her head, not smiling at his teasing tone. "No, it wasn't that. He just believed a woman's place was in the home, cooking, cleaning and raising kids."

Between sprinkling cupcakes, Devin dipped his finger into the frosting, licking off the rich confection. "Still, there's nothing wrong with a man wanting to come home to an orderly house and a hot meal," he argued.

She looked up at him, her eyes intense. "You don't believe a woman can handle a career and a family?"

"I didn't say that." Devin stared at her, seeing the stubborn tilt to her chin and the fire in her eyes. "Why are you getting so defensive all of a sudden?"

She looked away, grabbing the last of the cupcakes. "Let's just drop it, okay?"

His confetti shaker hit the counter hard, and Lilianne jumped, her gaze jerking back to his. "No, it's not okay," he said heatedly. He propped his hands on his waist. "Don't place all men in the same category, Lily. I realize Michael had certain beliefs where women were concerned." He swiped a hand through the air. "Hell, look at his mother. She doted on her husband and children. Michael was brought up in a household where his mother treated the men like kings and she was expected to be submissive. Did he expect you to be the same way?"

"Just drop it, Devin," she said through her teeth.

"Dammit, answer me!"

"Yes!" she shouted in frustration. "He expected me to be the perfect housewife, hostess and mother. When Jason started school and I told him I wanted to go back to work, he wouldn't let me."

"Wouldn't let you?" he asked quietly.

Lilianne started to clean up the mess in front of her, anything to keep her hands busy. "He said no wife of his was going to work, so I stayed home, just like he wanted." Her words poured out of her seemingly of their own will, having been bottled up for so long. "I cooked and cleaned and took care of the children until I couldn't handle it any longer. Then Jason went to school and I thought I'd go mad staying home all day." She looked up at Devin, the sponge in her hand stilling on the countertop. "I felt like I was losing my identity, Devin. My children were my life, but I needed to do something constructive with my days. I *wanted* to work."

"Did he finally agree?"

She laughed, choking on her bitterness. "Of course not. When I told him I was going to work with or without his permission he issued me an ultimatum—I could choose either career or marriage. Not both. I asked for a divorce, but he died before I filed the papers." Guilt replaced her anger. She resumed cleaning the counter, tossing the cooling racks into the sink, wiping up crumbs. Devin touched her arm and she looked up at him.

"I never knew, Lily. I'm sorry."

She shrugged, a sadness entering her eyes. "The year before he died we fought constantly. He didn't want me to work, but he spent more and more time at the office and away from home." She stared at the wall behind Devin, focusing on the floral wallpaper. "We were growing apart. It was getting to the point that we couldn't even have a civil conversation without bickering about something." She looked up at him. "All I wanted was a job, something constructive to do with my time. Was that so bad?"

"No, but for years you'd stayed home without wanting to work. Did you ever think that the suggestion might have come as a shock to Michael?"

"Yes. I gave him time to get used to the idea, but he became distant and cold. Whenever I tried to talk to him about it we'd end up arguing." She rubbed her forehead wearily with her fingers. "He was so against me working he pushed me over the edge with an ultimatum. He made me choose between him and my independence, Devin. It wasn't fair."

"No, it wasn't fair," he agreed softly. "He must have felt like he was losing control of the situation to take a risk like that. You and the kids were everything to him. He loved you, Lily—you know that."

"And I loved him. That never changed," she said adamantly. "We just became two separate people with different ideals. Just because I wanted to work didn't mean I didn't want to be a wife and mother, too. He wouldn't allow me to do both."

His fingers brushed her cheek. "I always thought you had too much fire for your own good." His gaze slowly dropped to her lips.

Lilianne's breath shortened and her fingers curled into a tight fist. She told herself to step away, but her body wouldn't obey the command. The pad of his thumb caressed her jaw, filling her with a hot, desperate need.

His eyes turned dark and sultry, his voice husky. "Let me taste that fire, Lily." With a single step he closed the gap between them.

Lilianne didn't move, couldn't move. Devin's large hands framed her face with a tenderness that touched her heart. He pulled her mouth up to his at the same time he lowered his head. Bursts of pleasure seared her when his lips melded with hers. Closing her eyes, she parted her lips, allowing his tongue to slide into her mouth. He kissed her like she'd never been kissed before, his lips and tongue a masterful blend of giving and taking.

Devin took his sweet time to sample every taste, every texture of her mouth. His tongue flicked over hers, and she returned the caress, sending a shaft of fire straight to his loins. Instantly, his body craved far more than this kiss could give.

Lilianne's head swam in a fog of desire. Devin angled her head, deepening the kiss even further. Moaning, she swayed into him, pressing her breasts intimately to his chest.

The doorbell sounded in the background. Devin heard it and silently cursed the intruder. Pulling away, he looked down at Lilianne's flushed face. Her breath came out in short pants and her eyes were glazed with passion. He swore again.

Devin shook her lightly, trying to snap her out of her daze. "Someone is at the door, Lily."

"Cupcakes," she mumbled, touching her wet lips.

There was a loud knock on the screen door. Devin glanced over his shoulder, then back at Lily. "Now isn't the time to worry about cupcakes."

"Yoo-hoo, anybody home?" a female voice called.

"Carolyn is here for the cupcakes," Lilianne said tonelessly. "I still have to put them in the box." Stepping away from Devin's touch, she began placing the remaining cupcakes in the small flat box. She looked at Devin, to find him regarding her strangely. "Would you please answer the door?"

Devin looked as though he wanted to say something, but didn't. Wheeling about, he walked out of the kitchen to the front door.

Closing her eyes, a shudder rippled through Lilianne's body. Who would have thought a man's kiss could make her tremble to the depths of her soul? She'd wanted to tear off his shirt and touch the hard planes of his body, explore the toned muscles that made up the man. Her body's instantaneous response to him was almost shameful—and delicious, she admitted. Like nothing she'd ever felt before. How could she face him without thinking about the heat of his tongue stroking her mouth, the way her breasts had been pressed against his hard chest?

"Hello, Lilianne," Carolyn said as she breezed into the kitchen, Devin tailing her. "I'm sorry I stopped by so early, but you were on my way to Marilyn's. I thought you might have the cupcakes done by now."

If Carolyn had stopped by any later she would have found her and Devin in an even more heated embrace, Lilianne was sure. If it weren't for Carolyn's timely interruption she'd have probably been begging Devin to take her to bed. God, she must be one frustrated woman!

"They're done. I just need to put them in the box for you." Lilianne could feel Devin's eyes on her back, possibly tracing the notches in her bare spine. Her hand became nerveless, and the last cupcake slipped from her clumsy fingers. She tried to save it from death on the floor and caught it, upside down, in the palm of her hand, a glob of frosting squishing between her fingers.

"Damn," she swore, staring at the cupcake and the mess in her hand.

"Oh, my," Carolyn said, placing her hand over her mouth.

Devin chuckled.

Lilianne glared at him, knowing his amusement was at her expense.

"If you don't mind, I'll just take these cupcakes and get going. Thanks for your help and support, Lilianne." Carolyn picked up the box and backed out of the kitchen.

Devin's chuckle deepened.

"What's so funny?" She started toward him, stalking him into the corner of the counter.

"You." Devin's mouth straightened, but laughter still lurked in the depths of his eyes. "You're so cute when you're mad."

"You think so?"

"Absolutely."

Slowly, she began peeling back the liner from the cupcake. The sticky frosting held it fast to her palm, enabling her to complete the task with one hand. Keeping her eyes on Devin's face, she closed her palm around the cake, squishing it and the frosting in her hand and between her fingers. Her lips curled into a playful smile.

Devin saw the wicked gleam in her eyes and knew she wasn't about to let him pass unscathed. "I wouldn't do what you're thinking if I were you."

She did, and it felt *so* good. Her hand shot out and rubbed the sticky, gooey cake over his jaw and cheek. He tried to back off, but the counter wouldn't give. She pressed forward, trying to avoid his hands, managing to cover his cheeks, chin, nose and mouth in chocolate before he manacled her wrists. She threw her head back and laughed, feeling young and silly and not caring. He'd deserved it, the scoundrel.

Devin smiled down at Lily, a flash of white teeth back-dropped against a chocolate-coated face. "Ahh, Lily, you shouldn't have done that."

She hooted with laughter, tears of mirth coming to her eyes. "Why not? I feel a whole lot better."

Pulling at her wrists, he brought her in close. "Because you're going to have to suffer the consequences."

Lilianne had mixed feelings about those consequences, even before he started lowering his head. One part of her wanted to lean into his strength and open up to him. Her heart, however, rang out a warning bell. This wasn't a game any longer. Something deep within her told her to be cautious, to tread lightly before she fell hard for Devin—if it wasn't already too late.

"C'mere, Lily," he said, his voice low and sexy.

She didn't move. A giggle caught in her throat when she looked at his face. A piece of cake hung from the tip of his nose.

The fingers encircling her wrists slid to her hand and he interlocked her sticky fingers with his. He coaxed her closer and she obeyed.

Lilianne gasped when he kissed her, his kiss a concoction of chocolate and male essence. He kissed her slowly, deeply, until her knees began to buckle and he had to let go of her hands and cup her buttocks to steady her. At the same time she wrapped her arms around his neck. The kiss went on forever, it seemed, until the slamming of the front screen door jarred her back to reality. They jumped apart, looking guilty and covered in chocolate cupcake.

Jason came barging into the kitchen. "Mom, can I—" He stopped, staring at her peculiarly. Then he switched his gaze to Devin and frowned. "What happened to you guys? Looks like you got slimed with chocolate."

Lilianne smiled, feeling the stickiness on her face, which had come from Devin's kiss. She looked down at her hands, then Devin's coated with mashed cupcake. Devin stared at her, lifting a brow as if to say, "How do you plan to get out of this one?"

Lilianne smiled at Jason. "We, uh, were just eating a cupcake."

"You guys sure are messy. You can hardly see Uncle Devin's face. You'd be dragging me up to the tub if I ate a cupcake like that."

"It was so good, we got a little carried away," Lilianne said.

Jason shrugged, as if how they ate a cupcake was of no consequence to him. "Can I have a dollar? The ice cream man's here."

"I think I have an extra dollar, Tiger," Devin said. He went to pull out his wallet, then remembered the cake on his hands. He turned and washed them in the sink.

Lilianne stared, horrified to see bits of chocolate cake ringing the back of his neck where her hands had been. Jason appeared not to notice and simply waited patiently for Devin to give him a dollar. He skipped happily from the room.

"You, ah, have cake on the back of your neck," she said.

"Wouldn't surprise me." A smile twitched the corner of his mouth. "You have it all over your face."

"I guess I'd better go clean up." Chin high, she sashayed out of the kitchen.

Devin chuckled at the two large, chocolate handprints on her buttocks.

He washed his hands and face and dried them with a paper towel. While he waited for Lily to return, he started cleaning up the kitchen, wondering if she felt the intense feelings he did. He'd loved her for so long he didn't know if he could handle it if she didn't love him in return. Then again, he didn't want to lose her friendship. If he treaded carefully, he figured he could have both.

Ten minutes later the kitchen was spotless and Lilianne hadn't returned. He went in search of her and found her in her office, standing by the bookcase flipping through a wallpaper-pattern book. She looked clean, but she hadn't changed her shorts. He doubted she even knew she had two handprints on her fanny. He also knew she'd be horrified to find out she did.

"The kitchen is clean," he said, moving into the room.

Lilianne looked over her shoulder in surprise. She should have known better than to hope he'd left. He wasn't an easy man to dismiss. That he'd cleaned the kitchen surprised her even more. "Thanks. You didn't have to do that."

He shrugged off her appreciation. "I don't mind."

Lilianne replaced the book in its slot, feeling uneasy now that they were alone again. She didn't care for the seriousness settling over Devin, the way his eyes watched her every move.

"Lily, I think we need to talk." Devin thrust his hands into the pockets of his shorts.

"About what?" she asked lightly, her smile falsely bright.

"You know about what," he said.

She moved behind her desk, using it as a means to separate the two of them. "So we shared a kiss. What's the big deal?" She began cleaning off her desk, putting the letter opener in the drawer, rearranging her stapler and tape dispenser.

"It was more than a kiss, Lily, and you know it." He walked around the barrier of the desk until he stood next to her. She looked up at him and he thought he detected fear in her eyes. Of him? He didn't touch her as he went on. "My feelings for you are changing, Lily. I've always cared for you, even loved you, and I can't fight the feeling any longer."

Her hand trembled as she tucked a stray strand of hair behind her ear. He loved her? His confession shocked her. "I never knew," she whispered.

"Of course you never knew. I made damn sure of it. Michael was my best friend, Lily. I could never betray him that way." He shoved his fingers through his hair, his eyes searching hers. "Ever since his death I've agonized over my feelings for you. I don't want to trample on his memory and I don't want to replace him. But I can't stop the way I feel about you."

His eyes, so dark and sensual, made her heart beat frantically in her chest. He made her feel things she'd never experienced before—fluttering in her stomach, a warmth between her thighs. She swallowed to ease the dryness in her throat. "I care for you, too, but what's happening between us scares me."

"Why?"

How could she tell him the truth, that the thought of commitment to a man frightened her? "You're such a wonderful friend I don't want to risk losing you if things don't work out with us. You're too important to the children."

Propping his hip on the corner of her desk, Devin swung his leg back and forth. "First and foremost, I'll always be your friend. We already know we're compatible. We get along great, but I want to take our relationship one step further so we can explore these feelings we have for one another."

Her eyes widened, an innocence touching her eyes. "You mean you want to become lovers?"

"Possibly." He smiled. "But for now I'll be happy knowing you'll see me exclusively."

Confused by her conflicting feelings, she chewed on her thumbnail. "I don't want to get tied down to another man."

"I'm not asking you to marry me." Not yet, anyway, Devin thought. Picking up a stray paper clip, he rolled it between his fingers. He'd gotten a brief taste of her attitude toward marriage earlier, and it hadn't been a pleasant one. She associated marriage and commitment with being ruled by a man, something she was fiercely against.

"I need space and my independence," Lilianne stated pointedly.

"I can respect that," he said easily.

She looked at him warily and started to lower herself to her chair. Halfway there, Devin grabbed her arm.

"You have two chocolate handprints on your fanny," he said, grinning.

"Oh."

Devin pulled her into the harbor of his thighs. She came without resisting, a positive sign. Setting his large hands on her hips, his fingers flexed into her soft flesh. "We'll take things slowly, Lily, and if you aren't comfortable with the direction they're heading, we'll go back to being just friends."

Resting her hands on his broad shoulders, she looked down at him. "Is that possible?"

He bestowed her with a dazzling smile. "Anything is possible."

"Okay, we'll try it your way."

Five

"Promise us you'll pretend like you don't know us at the dance, Mom," Elizabeth said from the back seat of the Volvo.

Lilianne looked over her shoulder at her daughters, catching Devin's smile of amusement on the way. "I plan on hugging and kissing both of you at least once an hour."

"Mom!" Emily said, horrified.

Devin looked in the rearview mirror, catching Emily's reflection. "She'll do no such thing. I'm going to keep her busy, remember?"

"Thank goodness you came along, Uncle Devin," Elizabeth said in relief.

Looking at Devin, Lilianne smiled. Things hadn't changed much between them since their discussion, except Devin now felt he had the liberty to kiss her or touch her when he wanted to. He did both often, not that she was complaining. It had been a long time since a man had showered her with such attention and affection, and she was enjoying it. The kids loved him being around and never questioned the frequency of his visits.

Devin drove the Volvo into the school parking lot, taking a slot in the front row. Before he could put the car into park the girls were scrambling out.

"From here on, you don't know us, Mother," Elizabeth said sternly.

Lilianne crossed her fingers over her heart as a promise, a gesture her children took seriously. "I promise I won't say a word to you all night long unless you approach me first."

"Deal."

Lilianne watched Elizabeth and Emily walk away. They'd both worn stylish dresses, the new ones she'd bought for them a week before. Their hair shone gold in the evening dusk and hung past their shoulder blades in the back. Elizabeth had left hers straight, while Emily's bounced with soft waves, an effect achieved with Lilianne's hot curlers.

Devin locked the car and grabbed Lilianne's hand, weaving their fingers together. She looked at him, her eyes shimmering. "They're growing up so fast," she said quietly. "Two more years and they'll be in high school. And then they'll be dating!"

Devin squeezed her hand as they followed at a discreet distance behind the twins. "Don't worry. I'll screen their dates."

She grinned, imagining Devin giving one of the girl's dates a stern lecture. "I wish Michael could be here to see them. He'd be so proud."

"Do you miss him, Lily?"

She looked down at her high heels crunching into the graveled parking lot. That was a hard question to answer. She had grieved when Michael died, because he'd been her husband and the father of her children. Sometimes she missed him when she woke up alone at night, but lately she'd begun to wonder if it was actually Michael himself she missed or if it was the warmth of a man cuddled up to her in the night. A man to chase away her fears and reassure her she was doing a good job with the children.

"I miss him at times like this," she admitted. "I know he would have enjoyed seeing the children grow up." She looked at Devin. His mahogany hair was attractively tousled and his eyes sparkled. He'd worn a pair of new jeans that outlined the leanness of his waist and the hardness of his thighs. The respectable blue-and-red-striped shirt he wore clung to his shoulders and chest. "How about you? Do you miss him?" she asked.

Hand in hand, they walked up the stairs to the auditorium. "Yes." Michael had been snatched from their lives so abruptly, in such a devastating way, Devin still felt the loss of his death. "I miss the easy friendship we shared. He was like a brother to me."

Lilianne paused at the door and turned to him. "Do you think he approves of us being together?" she asked softly.

Devin understood Lily's need for reassurance. How often had he spent a sleepless night staring at the ceiling, wondering the same thing? "I don't know for certain, but I think Michael would be happy knowing you found someone who loves you and the children. He often told me he trusted me with his life. I'm sure he'd trust me with his family."

She smiled at him, that soft, sweet smile that made him want to give her the moon. "Thank you," she said.

He squeezed her hand, knowing somehow he'd relieved both their minds of a heavy burden. He opened the metal door to the auditorium and music blared out at them. He looked over at Lilianne as two boys squeezed past him to get in. "I can't believe you talked me into this."

She tugged his hand. "Come on, it'll be fun."

Time passed quickly. Lilianne and Devin monitored the dance from a distance. For the most part the kids were good. Occasionally Devin would see a girl and a boy sneak off to neck. He'd give them five minutes, then drag them back to the dance. They grumbled, but obeyed.

Devin danced with Lilianne and the other women chaperons, having as good a time as the kids. The loud music nearly made him deaf and made normal conversation with Lilianne impossible.

"I need some fresh air," Lilianne said, breathing hard after dancing a fast dance with Devin. "I'm going to step outside for a bit."

Before Devin could reply, one of Elizabeth's friends grabbed his hand and tugged him toward the hardwood dance floor. Grinning, he waved at Lilianne.

Outside, a light breeze stirred, enough to cool her off. The sky was clear and bright stars shone like diamonds against black velvet. After a few minutes she went back inside. The lights had been turned low and a slow ballad played over the loudspeakers. She stood at the doorway, letting her eyes adjust to the dimness.

"Wanna neck?" a deep voice asked from behind her.

A shiver raced down Lilianne's spine, and the peaks of her breasts hardened. She spun around and found herself in Devin's arms. "Absolutely not!" she protested, a smile on her lips.

He pulled her deeper into the shadows, his eyes gleaming wickedly. His body picked up the slow, sensual beat of the music, rubbing against hers. "The girls said to keep you busy. What better way to keep you busy than by giving you long, slow kisses?"

Lilianne's breathing shortened and her stomach dropped a couple of inches. "I don't think this is what they had in mind." Resting her palms on his muscled chest, she tried leaning back. He only held her tighter. "Need I remind you we're the chaperons here? What kind of example would we be setting by necking?"

"Let me show you." Two steps back and he had her pinned against the cool brick wall. His mouth found hers easily, parting her lips so his tongue could explore the heated depths within. Her hands crept around his neck, her fingers running through his thick hair.

Lilianne heard boys' voices, but nothing could penetrate the fog of desire clouding her mind while Devin kissed her. He had incredible lips, and the things he did with his tongue were absolutely sinful. He knew when to soften a kiss and he detected the precise moment she wanted more, and complied. His body moved to the beat of the music, his hips gyrating into hers in a slow rhythm that made her tremble.

The voices became louder, then stopped. Devin came up for air and turned his head, spotting two young boys staring at them. Silently he cursed his lack of control.

"Hey, Mrs. Austin is kissing one of the other chaperons," one of the boys squealed, hurrying off to the crowd of kids in the middle of the dance floor. The other boy quickly followed, but not before he looked over his shoulder and grinned at Devin.

In less than a minute the whole auditorium knew that Mrs. Austin, Elizabeth and Emily's mother, had been necking with Mr. McKay. Although most of the kids snickered when Lilianne and Devin emerged from the shadows, Elizabeth and Emily looked mortified to the very tips of their low-heeled pumps.

"At least I kept my promise not to talk to them," Lilianne said, blushing from all the eyes trained on her.

"I don't think it matters much anymore." Devin kept a smile pasted on his face and tried acting like nothing out of the ordinary had happened. He was going to strangle the kid with the big mouth.

The DJ put on another song and announced a ladies' choice. The girls grabbed partners, and the incident was soon forgotten.

Elizabeth and Emily sulked on the way home from the dance.

"Mother, how *could* you?" Elizabeth said.

"I've never been more embarrassed in my whole life," Emily added.

"I think you guys will survive," Devin said sternly.

Lilianne stared at Devin, not knowing whether to be shocked or pleased at his authoritative tone. She had to take into account the twins' feelings about the whole situation. Sure, they'd been embarrassed, but did it bother them knowing that their mother was entering into a deeper relationship with their uncle Devin? Did they even realize the implication of Devin's kissing her?

"Girls, I'm sorry if we embarrassed you." Lilianne twisted in her seat so she could see them better.

"If you want to kiss Uncle Devin, fine. But don't do it where you're going to get caught," Elizabeth said, crossing her arms over her chest.

"Especially by one of our friends," Emily added.

Lilianne cleared her throat, feeling awkward with the next question. She forced it out. "Does it bother you if, ah, Uncle Devin and I kiss?"

The twins looked at each other, as if silently consulting over Lilianne's question. Then they looked back at her. Emily shrugged. "No. Are you going to marry Uncle Devin?"

Lilianne ignored Devin's sharp glance. "No, sweetheart. Uncle Devin and I are just good friends."

Devin wanted to dispute that, but now was not the time.

"Oh," Emily said quietly. "We wouldn't mind if you did. It would be great to have Uncle Devin as a dad."

Don't dig me in any deeper, Emily, Lilianne thought silently. "I'm glad you feel that way. Uncle Devin will always be around for you, honey. You know that, don't you?"

"Yeah."

Lilianne turned quickly in her seat to stare out the windshield before any more uncomfortable questions could be fired her way.

Devin as her husband? Although the thought made her insides warm like sitting before a cozy fire, it frightened the hell out of her. The kids needed a father, not a part-time uncle, but what did she need? Being a woman, she wouldn't mind sleeping next to him at night, making love, then snuggling, but what would happen in the light of day? She imagined herself pregnant again and blanched. If she had another baby she'd be expected to stay home, take care of it, be a housewife. The career she'd built for herself would once again become a distant dream.

She didn't need a man, she reasoned. They were nice for companionship and warming your bed, but she wouldn't allow herself to get dependent on one ever again. Once had been enough.

Devin curled his fingers around the steering wheel, resisting the urge to reach over and grab Lilianne's hands, which were twisting together in her lap. She bit her bottom lip, looking deep in thought. He knew the direction her mind was racing, not hard to figure since he'd seen her reaction to Emily's question of marriage.

Normally Devin considered himself a patient man. He'd shown three long years of restraint in confessing his feelings to Lilianne, but now that she knew how he felt about her, he wanted more. He wanted to share her life, laugh with her, argue with her so he could see her fire, and he wanted to make love to her, feel his baby grow in her belly.

Turning into Lilianne's street, Devin knew he wouldn't be satisfied with kisses and stolen moments forever. After a long day at work he wanted to come home to a wife and family, sit at the dinner table and share the day's events. He could do that now, but it wasn't the same. He'd be spending his nights alone in his own bed while Lilianne slept in hers.

* * *

Three days later, on the evening of the Meadowbrook Development Project opening Devin arrived half an hour early to pick up Lilianne.

Jason answered the door, excited to see him. Devin ruffled his hair as he walked into the house. "Hey, Tiger, where's your mom?"

Jason wrinkled his nose at him. "In her bedroom getting ready."

Devin tweaked his nose. "You all packed and ready to go to Rusty's?"

Giggling, Jason rubbed his nose. "Yep. Rusty's mom bought him the Teenage Mutant Ninja Turtle video, and we're going to watch it tonight."

"Are Elizabeth and Emily here?" Devin asked, looking around the living room, listening for girlish laughter. Nothing.

Jason shook his head. "Nope. They're at a slumber party at Kathleen Dorman's house."

Devin smiled. Great, just as planned. "Why don't you go get your bag and I'll see if your mom's ready." Walking down the hall to Lilianne's bedroom, Devin knocked on the closed door.

"Come in, honey," Lilianne called.

Devin liked the sound of that endearment. He grinned as he stepped into her bedroom. "Honey?" he teased.

Lilianne looked up as she smoothed her dress over her hips. "Oh, hi, Devin," she said, her voice breathless. "I thought you were Jason."

Devin's mouth went dry at the sight of her. She looked gorgeous and radiant in a deep blue dress that clung to her generous curves. The sleeves were short and pulled down off her arms so her shoulders were bare. Lace bordered the plunging neckline. Sheer black stockings tinted her legs and black leather pumps encased her feet. Her hair had been arranged into an old-fashioned topknot. The effect softened her features and made her look young and romantic. Shimmering silver-and-blue earrings dangled from her ears, nearly touching her shoulders.

The dress, alluring and tempting, brought forth forbidden images of stripping it away to discover what lay beneath. Devin's dark eyes scanned the length of her as his imagination went into overdrive, picturing skimpy, lace panties and creamy, silken flesh.

Lilianne twirled for Devin's inspection. "What do you think?" she asked, anticipation making her eyes sparkle.

"I think you look stunning and too damned seductive. What do you say we drop Jason off, then come back home and forget the opening?"

"Devin!"

"Hey," he said, shrugging, "it was just an idea. Can't blame a man for trying."

No, she couldn't, because she felt the same way. For the past couple of weeks all she could think of was him and the depth of their affection for one another. The next step in their relationship would push her over the edge, and she wasn't sure if she was ready to fall. She picked up a crystal atomizer Michael had given her one year for her birthday and noticed how her hand shook. Before she could push the sprayer, Devin took it from her.

"Nervous?" he murmured, looking into her eyes.

She nodded. "A little. Meadowbrook is my first big account. There should be a pretty big turnout."

Lifting the atomizer, Devin sprayed a fine layer of perfume on her neck. Holding her gaze, his finger lightly touched the still-wet spot, then slid down the graceful slope of her throat to the cleavage spilling from the dress. Her breathing deepened. His eyes dropped to her lips, and they automatically parted. One large hand curved over the roundness of her breast while the other slipped to her waist to pull her in close. Her eyes fluttered shut as he slowly lowered his head.

"Mom, are you ready to go yet?" Jason asked impatiently through the closed door.

Lilianne jumped back out of Devin's embrace, appalled that she'd come so close to letting him seduce her with her son in the house.

Devin wanted to howl in frustration. Instead, he cursed vividly, making Lilianne's eyes widen. "We'll be right there, Jason," he growled.

"Okay, but hurry," Jason said.

"You're pushing it, kid," Devin said under his breath. He combed his fingers through his hair. "There are too many damned interruptions."

Lilianne had a hand over her frantically beating heart. She used it to straighten out the bodice of her dress. "You don't get much peace and quiet with kids around."

"We'll see about that," Devin murmured under his breath as Lilianne walked to the bed to retrieve her purse.

The reception for Meadowbrook was in full swing when Devin and Lilianne arrived. There were groups of men in business suits and women in cocktail dresses discussing the merits of Lilianne's interior decorating.

Devin looked around the large reception area. It was a tasteful blend of sophistication and warmth. Lithograph pictures hung on the walls, and silk plants sat on marble pillars.

Lilianne gave Devin a brief tour. He noted how each of the offices had been individually decorated. By the time he'd seen the whole complex he was suitably impressed.

"You did this by yourself?" Devin asked. He grabbed two glasses of champagne off a passing tray and handed one to Lilianne.

Nodding, Lilianne took a sip of the bubbly liquid. "Yes. It took months, but I'm quite pleased with it."

"You should be. You've done an incredible job."

Lilianne's chest swelled with pride. Devin's praise warmed her. She'd completed plenty of small projects, but this accomplishment ranked her as a true professional. She'd already begun receiving referral calls just on the basis of someone seeing the redecoration of this office.

"I'm very proud of you," Devin said, his voice low and intimate around the crowd of people. "I never doubted you could do it."

She smiled at him, feeling a ray of sunshine from the inside out. "Thank you, Devin."

"There you are, Lilianne," a deep voice boomed through the reception area. A small, round man emerged from the throng of people, trailed by his wife, a tall blonde with endlessly long legs.

"Edward." Lilianne stepped forward and accepted the kiss Edward planted on her cheek. She nodded politely to Marcella, whom she'd met before.

Lilianne introduced Edward Livingston, her client, to Devin, and they shook hands.

"Lilianne's quite a gal," Edward said, slapping Devin jovially on the back. Devin was barely able to keep the contents of his glass from sloshing onto the new carpet. "She sat for hours with me discussing just the right colors and details for each office. She was worth every penny I paid her."

"I think her rates just went up." Devin winked at Lilianne.

They spent another two hours being introduced to clients and friends of Edward's. Lilianne smiled and accepted everyone's gracious comments on her work. By the time the night ended, she was exhausted, but pleased with herself.

As soon as she and Devin walked into the house, Lilianne slipped off her high heels. They'd left a lamp on low in the living room, and she tossed her purse onto the couch and turned to Devin. She felt heady with success... and love, she realized, looking into his eyes.

"Thank you for going with me."

"You bet." Shrugging out of his suit coat, Devin draped it over the recliner. He pulled at his tie, loosening it enough to take it off.

All of a sudden, nerves began to flutter in Lilianne's stomach. In the shadows of the lone light Devin looked virile and masculine. She watched as he released the first two buttons of his shirt, revealing the strong column of his throat and tufts of dark curling hair covering his chest.

He came to her and cupped her cheek in his palm, caressing her lips with the pad of his thumb. His eyes grew so dark they looked nearly black. "I don't want to go home tonight and I don't want to settle for a few kisses. I want you, Lily. I want you so badly I can't think straight anymore."

Lily closed her eyes against the feelings raging inside her. If she said yes to Devin she would forever alter their relationship. If she said no, she knew she would always regret it. She loved him, and the strong feelings coming from her heart and soul told her this was right. Taking his hand, she silently led him down the hallway to her bedroom. She turned the bedside lamp on low, then faced him.

Devin finished unbuttoning his shirt and shrugged out of it, all the while watching Lilianne. She crossed the room and stood before her vanity mirror. Her hands shook as she removed her earrings and laid them carefully on the table.

Devin came up behind her, running his hands up and down her arms. He caught her gaze in the mirror. "How long has it been?" he asked gently, already knowing the answer.

"Since Michael died," she said quietly.

His fingers traced the neckline of the dress until he came to the zipper in the back. "Three years is a long time."

Her eyes glazed over with desire. "I never realized how long until now."

Smiling tenderly, Devin unzipped her dress, tracing her spine with his finger all the way down to her buttocks. Palms flattened, he smoothed his hands back up to her shoulders, never breaking eye contact in the mirror. His fingers curled around the edge of the dress and slowly pulled the sleeves down her arms and over her hips, letting the material fall into a silky pool at her feet.

Lilianne hugged her arms over her breasts, thankful the light was dim so he couldn't see the stretch marks on her stomach. Once he peeled her panty hose off, however, there would be nothing left to conceal them.

"Lily, drop your arms," he said huskily. "I want to see you."

She swallowed her pride. "Devin, I don't pretend to have an incredibly toned, young body. I carried twins and it shows."

He skimmed his hands up her ribs, leaving quivering flesh in their wake. "Do you honestly think I care about that?"

"I'm sure you're used to thin, perfectly shaped women. I'm far from it."

"I don't want anyone but you, Lily." He pulled her arms back to her sides, his expression growing hungry at the sight of her full breasts. "I think you're incredibly beautiful." Watching her expression in the mirror, he took the soft mounds in his hands, bringing the nipples to life.

Moaning, Lilianne leaned into his chest. Bursts of pleasure started in her breasts and traveled down between her thighs. Her heart pounded in her ears and every nerve ending in her body tingled.

Kneeling in front of her, Devin removed her hose and panties, kissing her flesh as he bared it. He paid special attention to her stretch marks, running his tongue over them until her fingers wove into his hair to tug him back up.

He pulled out the pins holding the mass of hair on her head, letting the tresses tumble around her shoulders. Burying his hand in the silky tresses, he brought her mouth to his and kissed her slowly, deeply, swirling his tongue against hers.

Lilianne's heart swelled with love for Devin. Her body responded to his like a match to kindling, spreading wildfire throughout her body. Arching her back, she brought her breasts against his chest and rubbed, gasping at the feel of his coarse body hair tickling her sensitive nipples.

Devin was hard and aching. He didn't think he could wait much longer to be inside the warmth and softness of Lilianne's body. Taking her hand, he tugged her toward the bed. He tossed the frilly pillows to the floor, heedless of where they landed. Yanking the satin bedspread and blanket to the foot of the bed, he pushed Lilianne on top of the cool sheet. It took him less than a minute to shuck his shoes, socks, pants and underwear. He came down on top of her, his hard manhood cradled in the cove of her thighs. Running his hand up her thigh, he closed his mouth over hers, kissing her with raw passion. In the next instant he was slowly sliding into her.

Lilianne gasped, lifting her hips for Devin's penetration. He felt so good and so right, his body perfectly aligned with hers. Opening her eyes, she stared into his face, watching the myriad expressions as he thrust deep inside her. Love and adoration shone from his eyes, and pure pleasure curled his mouth.

Soon Lilianne was lost in exquisite ecstasy. With every rhythmic movement of Devin's body a pressure built deep inside her until it finally surfaced. Her nerves exploded into a million shattering pieces, and she cried out, vaguely aware of Devin calling her name, of his body jerking hard into hers.

He collapsed on top of her, and she reveled in the feeling of his weight and warmth. Her hands stroked his back, holding him close.

He lifted his head and stared down at Lilianne's flushed face. He'd never seen a more beautiful woman. Lowering his head, he kissed her slowly and deeply. When he looked at her again her eyes were glazed, her lips swollen and wet.

"I love you," he said, his voice husky.

She smiled, dragging her hands up the slope of his back. "I love you, too."

He shook his head, knowing she'd misunderstood him. "No, I mean I'm in love with you."

She cocked her head to the side. "Isn't that the same thing?"

"Maybe it is to you. I'm not talking about a friendship kind of love, Lily. I love you with everything I am. Like a husband loves a wife."

Lilianne's body stiffened and her hands stilled in his hair at the nape of his neck. Old doubts resurfaced, shadowing her eyes. Her feelings of love for Devin certainly went deeper than friendship, but that didn't mean she wanted to marry him. Suddenly she felt crushed and suffocated. Pushing at Devin's shoulders, she gave him a frantic look, and he rolled off of her.

I'm going too fast, Devin thought, cursing himself for his impatience. He gathered Lilianne to him, holding her close, but saying nothing more. What could he say? He'd poured his heart out to her, and although he knew Lilianne loved him as he loved her, she'd never admit it. She didn't want to be tied permanently to any man. It was as simple and as difficult as that. He didn't know if he could settle for less than marriage to her.

As the night evolved into morning, Devin made love to Lilianne twice more, one time fierce and hard, the other gentle and sweet. His heart became torn between having

Lily, yet knowing she'd never commit herself to marriage, no matter how strong and deep her feelings for him ran.

By morning, he'd made up his mind. He couldn't spend the rest of his life sneaking in and out of Lilianne's bed. He couldn't keep his true feelings about her from the kids, feeling guilty every time they caught them in a heated embrace. He wanted to be a real father to the children, giving them guidance and love without feeling as if he was intruding on Michael's memory.

He was going to take a gamble of a lifetime; all or nothing.

Six

Lilianne awoke feeling lazy and content. Her legs were entwined with Devin's and her head rested in the cradle of his arm and shoulder. Her body ached from the vigorous activities of the previous night, something she wasn't accustomed to. But, she reflected with a smile, she could easily *get* accustomed.

Lifting her head, she peered down into his face, finding his eyes open and looking at her. Smiling, she touched the dark stubble on his jaw. "Good morning," she murmured.

"Good morning, Lily."

He looked awfully serious and deep in thought for first thing in the morning. The pad of her finger ran over the furrows between his eyes, trying to smooth them out. Finally he smiled, then pulled her down for a quick kiss.

Lilianne clutched the sheet to her breasts, feeling self-conscious in the light of day. She ran a hand over her hair, knowing it was a mass of wild tangles. She never looked her best first thing in the morning.

"You look beautiful, Lily," Devin said, as if sensing her discomfort.

"You're a liar, but thank you, anyway. I always look terrible first thing in the morning."

"You look like a woman who's been well and truly loved."

Tumbling onto her back, she stretched lazily. "Ummm, I feel like it. I suppose we should rouse ourselves before the kids get home." She looked at him and grinned. "You know our luck with getting caught."

He came up on his elbow and trailed his hand from her neck to her breast, nudging the sheet aside. Cupping the silky flesh in his hands, he stroked his thumb over her nipple, watching as it responded. "I don't mind getting caught."

She grasped his wrist as his hand slid over her belly. "I'm not ready to explain our new relationship to the kids yet."

He withdrew his hand and his lashes lowered, veiling his mounting frustration. "I guess we'd better get up then." Sliding off the bed, he went into the bathroom, closing the door behind him.

As Lilianne dressed in a baggy T-shirt and an old pair of jeans, she wondered at Devin's cool attitude. This wasn't the man who'd made mad, passionate love to her the night before. He'd withdrawn from her, and it bothered her. Did he regret making love to her? Was she not what he'd expected? Shaking her head of the thoughts, she went to her vanity mirror.

One look confirmed her earlier suspicions. She was truly disheveled. Brushing out the tangles in her hair, she pulled it back into a ponytail. She went into the kids' bathroom and washed her face and brushed her teeth. Staring at her reflection, she noted a certain glow on her cheeks, a sparkle in her eyes. With a lightness to her step she went to the kitchen and started breakfast.

Devin emerged from the bathroom, the smell of sizzling bacon greeting him. He pulled on his underwear, then his pants and shirt. Looking at the bed, he took in the rumpled sheets, remembering Lily's uninhibited response to him the night before. She was everything he wanted in a woman and more. She had a gentle and kind nature, made him laugh, was sensible and hardworking, and passionate enough to keep him well satisfied.

Devin walked barefoot into the kitchen, heading straight for the coffeepot. Bringing down a mug from the cupboard, he filled it with the rich, aromatic brew. He leaned his hip against the counter and watched Lilianne scramble eggs and flip pancakes. He marveled at her ease in the kitchen, then remembered she'd had years of practice.

"How many pancakes do you want?" she asked, bestowing him with a dazzling smile.

Breakfast was the last thing on his mind. His stomach twisted with anxiety, knowing he'd be confronting Lilianne with marriage in a short while. "Two," he answered, taking a sip of coffee.

"You're not very hungry for a man who worked awfully hard last night," she teased.

"It's not food I'm hungry for," he said, straight-faced. He was hungry for much more. Permanency, intimacy, family. He wanted to set down roots and start a new life with Lily by his side, making him complete.

Lilianne flipped two pancakes onto a plate, along with some scrambled eggs and bacon. She handed it to him. "Butter and syrup are on the table."

"Thanks," he murmured. His stomach growled as the delicious smells assaulted his nostrils. Okay, so he was a little hungry for food.

Devin ate everything on his plate and even finished the leftover scrambled eggs and bacon. Taking his plate to the sink, he rinsed it off, then grabbed the coffeepot and filled both their mugs. When he again sat down next to Lilianne, he gazed thoughtfully into the black depths of his mug, garnering the courage to broach the subject of marriage.

"Are you all right?" Lilianne asked, frowning at him. She reached out and touched his arm, drawing his gaze to hers.

Devin drew in a deep breath. "Lilianne, about last night..."

Lilianne jerked back her hand as if she'd been burned. "Do you regret what happened?"

He smiled gently. "No, not at all. Just the opposite, in fact. I want what we shared last night every night."

Lilianne visibly relaxed. She ate the last bite of bacon and placed her fork on her plate. "Last night was wonderful, Devin, but when the kids are home I don't think it would be a good idea if you stayed the night."

"That's just the point. I want to spend every night with you."

Her coffee mug halted midway to her mouth. "You mean you want to live with us?"

"In a way." He watched confusion settle over her features. "Do you love me, Lily?"

Her delicate shoulders slumped and her eyes softened perceptibly. "You know I do."

"Enough to marry me?"

Lilianne sucked in a breath. "Devin, I do love you, very much, but I'm not looking for marriage. I told you that."

"Yeah, I know what you told me. Unfortunately I want more. I don't want a bunch of one-nighters, and I don't want to sneak around the children."

"But that's all I can give you, Devin. I can't give you more."

The dark centers of his eyes turned stormy. "Can't or won't, Lily?"

"Both. I love my life the way it is. I come and go when I please. I depend on no one but myself."

"I don't want to take anything from you. I'm proud of you and your business. I'd never demand that you put one before the other."

Her lashes lowered, veiling the skepticism in them. "Why can't we just keep things the way they are?"

Abruptly he stood. Bracing his palms on the table, he leaned toward her. "Because, dammit, I want to sleep with you every night without having to worry about sneaking out before the kids wake up. I want to eat breakfast with the family, and I want to share dinner and discuss the kids' day at school and your day designing. I want to be a real father to the children and, most especially, I want to have a baby with you."

Lilianne gasped, her hand fluttering to the neck of her T-shirt. "I'm too old to have another baby, Devin."

Straightening, he jammed his hands on his hips. "Hell, Lily, you're only thirty-six, hardly near the age of menopause."

"I don't want another baby," she said adamantly, feeling at a disadvantage because she had to look up at him. "I don't want the responsibility of having to stay home all day and take care of a baby while you're out working and the other kids are in school. I'd go crazy!"

"No one says you have to stay home and be strictly a mother. Wasn't it you who mentioned having a family and a career? You can do both and still be happy."

"No, Devin." She sighed, brushing the wispy bangs from her forehead. "I don't want to lose you, Devin, but I can't give you what you're asking."

He stared at her, a muscle in his jaw twitching. "You don't want to need me, Lily, but you do. There's nothing wrong or weak about that."

The authority in his words angered and provoked her. Jumping out of her seat, she jabbed her finger his way, coming precariously close to poking him in the chest. "I don't need you or any other man."

He locked his gaze with hers. "Then I guess it's best if I step out of your life," he said quietly.

Oh, God, what had she done? Lilianne panicked, thinking about how much she loved him and needed him, despite her angry words. "You promised me if things didn't work out between us we could still be friends."

He shook his head, his eyes full of regret. "I can't do it, Lily. I can't pretend we didn't share something rare and special. I love you so much it'll hurt too much to be near you, knowing I can never truly have you."

Lilianne cursed the tears burning in her eyes. Her heart felt like it was being ripped from her chest. "What about the kids?" she asked in a last-ditch effort.

"I'll still come by and see them." He rubbed the back of his neck and stared at the tiled floor. "I love all three of them like they were my own. There is no reason our differences should affect them."

"Don't do this to us, Devin." Lilianne realized she was pleading.

Devin's heart twisted, making the pain course throughout his entire body, but he didn't back down. "I have to. If I don't, I'll only come to resent the situation. I'm greedy, Lily. I want everything or nothing at all. If you ever change your mind, just let me know."

Lilianne lifted her chin high as he walked out of the dining room. She refused to beg anymore. She heard the front door open and close. "Damn you, Devin McKay, for making me care so much. I never wanted to love someone so much it felt like I was dying when they walked away," she whispered. "What am I going to do without you?"

"Happy birthday to you, happy birthday to you, happy birthday, dear Elizabeth and Emily, happy birthday to you!"

Devin clapped and cheered as, together, the twins blew out the thirteen candles on their birthday cake. He nudged Jason in the ribs, who sat next to him. "How about getting us each a big piece of cake?"

"Okay." Jason scrambled off his folding chair. "I better get there quick before Mom gives the corner pieces away."

As Jason raced for the cake, Devin glanced around Lilianne's backyard. Birthday streamers fluttered in the breeze and helium balloons tied to the porch posts strained against their bondage of ribbons. A table with condiments for the hot dogs and hamburgers sat beside the barbecue, covered with plastic now since most of the kids had eaten. The twins were in a circle with their friends, talking and giggling. His gaze finally settled on Lilianne, and his heart lurched, then began a fierce, painful throbbing.

She was wearing a pink blouse tucked into white jeans, and her hair fell in a riot of red-gold waves to her shoulders. She smiled perfunctorily at the children as she served them slices of cake, but she lacked her normal enthusiasm and cheer. It hurt to think he was responsible for this change in her.

Jason brought him a piece of cake, saving him from encountering Lily and seeing close up the dullness of her normally sparkling eyes.

"How come you hardly ever come over anymore?" Jason asked him. The boy shoveled a piece of cake into his mouth, waiting for Devin's answer.

Devin smiled, stiff and forced. "I come over, Tiger. I see you all the time."

Jason didn't look convinced. "You never come over when Mom's around, and you don't stay for dinner like you used to."

Devin's cake landed like lead in his stomach. "I've been busy at the shop."

Jason sighed, picking at his frosting. "Mom's been so grouchy lately. She's always yelling at us, and then she'll burst into tears and hug us and tell us she's sorry." He looked up at Devin, confusion making his brow pucker. "What's wrong with her?"

Devin pushed aside the guilt pulling at his conscience. "She's probably working too hard and she's tired."

Jason shook his head, a little man of wisdom. "I don't think so. Every time I walk into her office when she's supposed to be working she's just staring off into space."

Devin's gaze sought out Lily. He found her smiling at one of the twins' friends, but the smile didn't change the sadness lingering in her expression. His gut twisted when he thought about how much he missed her.

"You never talk to her anymore," Jason said quietly, swinging his legs back and forth under the chair. His expression guileless, he glanced up at Devin. "She always used to laugh and smile when you were around. How come that changed? Did you guys have a fight?"

Devin couldn't lie to Jason. "Yes, we had a...a disagreement, but it doesn't change the way I feel about you or your sisters."

Hanging his head, Jason resumed eating his cake. "I wish you and Mom would make up."

So did he. Devin had never spent a more miserable month in his life. He was beginning to regret his rash decision to stop seeing Lily, but then he realized it was more painful seeing her, knowing she'd never truly be his, rather than not seeing her at all. He thought of her so much he found himself daydreaming while at work. At night he couldn't sleep because he remembered too well the feel of her satin skin beneath his, the way her body responded to his touch. He missed holding her, kissing her, teasing her, talking to her. Even arguing with her.

He was a fool for thinking if he bowed out of her life and gave her room she'd change her mind about marriage. Her stubborn pride would never allow it.

Devin watched Lilianne take the remaining cake into the house. Turning to Jason, he asked, "Are you through with your cake?"

"Yeah," Jason said, handing Devin his plate. He eyed the piñata hanging from a porch beam. Elizabeth had grabbed a broom handle and was getting ready to take her turn trying to break it open. Jumping down from his chair, Jason ran to the end of the piñata line.

Devin chuckled, the sound gratifying to his own ears. When was the last time he'd laughed? He couldn't remember exactly, but he was certain it had been with Lily. He looked toward the house, knowing Lily was inside somewhere. He decided he wanted to see her, talk to her.

As Lilianne cleared the counter of party paraphernalia, then wrapped tinfoil around the leftover cake, she tried not to think of Devin sitting outside, so close, yet so far away. When she'd opened the door to him this afternoon and he'd politely said hello, then walked past her to accept the twins' hugs, her heart had shriveled.

Now her heart felt like a wound, raw and tender. She'd cried and grieved for Devin so much she didn't think she had any emotion left in her. His absence from her life hurt worse than anything she could have imagined, and that scared her witless. That meant dependency, something she refused to accept.

"How are you, Lily?"

Lilianne jumped at the rough yet gentle male voice behind her. The box of foil fell from her nerveless fingers to the floor. She pasted on a smile as she turned. "Just fine," she said brightly, sounding phony to her own ears. "And you?"

"Miserable. Lonely as hell. I miss you." Devin stooped and picked up the tinfoil, placing it on the counter. He met her eyes, so green and full of heartache. His insides tightened, holding back the urge to fold her in his embrace and shower his love on her.

Lilianne's eyes teared, hot and burning. "Don't, Devin. You're the one who asked for this, not me."

He stood, unbending, his expression hardening just a bit. "There is a solution to the problem."

Oh, yes, if only he knew how often she'd considered it! Lilianne turned from him before he could read the truth in her face. Sometimes, when the hurt got so bad and she wanted more than anything to be held in his arms, her cherished independence didn't count for much. Still, she couldn't bring herself to say the words "I need you," to end all the agony and torture ripping her soul to shreds.

"I never meant to hurt you, Lily," Devin said quietly, shoving his fingers into the pockets of his jeans. "I guess my pride is just as stubborn as yours."

I need you! she cried from the bottom of her soul, but the words wouldn't come. Instead, she turned back around and said in an even voice, "Thank you for coming today, despite everything."

He nodded curtly. "I would never miss the twins' birthday, Lily."

A young girl came into the kitchen, her face radiating her excitement. "Mrs. Austin, Elizabeth and Emily are getting ready to open their presents."

Lilianne managed a pleasant smile. "I'll be right there, Cindy."

Devin waited until the girl had left the kitchen. He looked at Lilianne, wishing he wasn't so greedy and could settle for less. "If you ever need me for anything, Lily, you have my number."

"Things aren't the same now," she said, suddenly angry.

Regret filled Devin's dark eyes. "I know, but right now that's all I can give you."

Lilianne watched Devin walk out of the kitchen. *That's all I can give you.* Now that she was on the receiving end of those words, she realized how horribly selfish they sounded.

"Mrs. Austin, Mrs. Austin!"

Lilianne lifted her head from the invoice she was writing

out and frowned at the distant voice calling her name. It sounded like Rusty.

"Mrs. Austin!"

Lilianne rose from her chair and walked out of the office toward the front hallway. Rusty flew through the screen door, his face beet-red and his chest heaving. Tears were streaming down his cheeks and his eyes were wide in fear.

She immediately rushed to him, thinking Jason had yet again provoked the boy—her son had become so rebellious lately. "What's wrong, Rusty?"

"It's Jason," he said between gulps of air. "We were riding our bikes and . . . and he . . ." He started to cry even harder.

Suddenly Lilianne could hear sirens in the distance. Fear ripped through her.

"Jason got hit by a car!" Rusty got out at last.

Lilianne's stomach heaved. She raced out of the house, running as fast as she could to the end of the street where an ambulance and two police cars had come to a stop. She pushed her way through all the gawking neighbors and kids. A scream lodged in her throat when she saw Jason lying unconscious on the pavement, two paramedics working over him. His arm was twisted at an odd angle, and blood ran from his nose. His bike lay in a mangled mess a few feet away.

Lilianne told the paramedics who she was, keeping her hysterics at bay. Her head swirled and adrenaline pumped through her as she accompanied Jason to the hospital, riding in the back of the ambulance by his side. He hadn't regained consciousness. The paramedics couldn't accurately assess any internal damage, leaving Lilianne to wonder if her son would even live.

At the hospital a crew immediately wheeled Jason into the emergency room. The nurses instructed Lilianne to wait in the lounge. The doctor would speak with her shortly, they said.

Lilianne paced the room, heedless of the curious stares cast her way. Horrible, unthinkable thoughts ran through her mind, expanding her chest in anxiety. She had to call someone to let them know what had happened. She dashed to a phone.

Strangely, the first number Lilianne dialed wasn't her parents or her brother's. The deep, smooth voice answering her call automatically soothed her frayed nerves.

"McKay's Body Works." Devin's voice was unenthusiastic after a long day spent priming and painting cars.

Lilianne closed her eyes, feeling a warmth instantly begin to curl through her body. How could she have gone so long without him?

"Hello?"

"Devin," Lilianne began, hiccuping. "I need you."

"Lily?"

The dam of emotions broke, bringing on a torrent of tears. Lilianne couldn't stop the deep sobs ripping from her throat. She'd been so calm and collected through the ordeal thus far, and now she needed someone to lean on, someone to share the pain.

"Lily, what's wrong?" Panic laced Devin's voice.

Lilianne corralled her emotions, dashing the tears off her face with the palm of her hand. "Jason's been hit by a car."

Devin sucked in a breath, then went on urgently. "Where are you?"

"St. Mary's Hospital."

"I'll be right there."

Lilianne continued to hold on to the receiver long after the line went dead, as if she could somehow absorb his strength that way. Then she called her parents and her brother, asking him if he'd pick up the girls from the house and keep them for the night.

Devin arrived twenty minutes later. As soon as he walked into the waiting room, Lilianne rushed into his open arms. Her eyes were puffy from crying and her body trembled with fear. Rocking her gently in his embrace, Devin stroked her hair, whispering, "Shh, sweetheart. Everything will be fine."

Lilianne burrowed closer into the warmth and support of his muscular chest. Her hiccups slowly receded as she breathed in the masculine scent of him.

"How is he?" Devin's hand caressed her back, relaxing her tense muscles.

Pulling away, Lilianne stared up at Devin. "I don't know. They immediately took him in and I haven't seen him since. The nurses won't tell me a thing."

He smiled grimly. "I know. The waiting is the hardest part. I'll be here with you."

Gratitude deepened the green of her eyes. "Thank you."

At last a doctor stepped into the waiting room, his eyes scanning the occupants.

Lilianne was sitting next to Devin on a green plaid couch, her head resting on his shoulder, her hand sheltered warmly in his. They stood as the doctor approached them.

"Mrs. Austin?"

"Yes," Lilianne answered worriedly. "How is Jason?" Behind her, Devin's hands rested on her shoulders, his fingers flexing.

The doctor reached out and touched her hand. "He broke his arm in three places and he has two cracked ribs. He also has a slight concussion."

Lilianne gasped, tears welling up in her eyes. She reached for Devin's hand on her shoulder and squeezed tight. She forced out the words lodged in her throat. "Is he going to be all right?"

"I think so. He didn't sustain any serious damage."

Lilianne closed her eyes and sent up a silent prayer of thanks. She felt Devin's body relax behind her.

The doctor went on, "However, we want to keep him here for a couple of days. Considering the speed the car was reportedly going when your son got hit, Jason is a very lucky young man. Things could have been much worse. He's a strong and healthy boy. He'll pull through just fine."

"Can we see him?" she asked anxiously.

"Of course. Come this way."

Lilianne and Devin followed the doctor down the hall to Jason's room. He left them there, asking that they stay only a few minutes.

Jason lay on the bed, his wheat-colored hair tousled around his face. A nasty-looking bruise discolored one cheek, and his left arm was plastered in a cast all the way from his fingers to his shoulder. He looked terribly pale and vulnerable.

Devin joined her at the side of Jason's bed, offering silent support.

Leaning over, she kissed her son's forehead. "I love you," she whispered.

Jason's eyes fluttered halfway open. "Mom?" he asked, his voice faint and raspy.

She smiled for his benefit, even as fresh tears filled her eyes. Tenderly she brushed a stray lock of hair from his brow. "Yes, sweetheart, it's me."

He swallowed, the effort making him wince in pain. "I'm sorry. I didn't see the car."

"Oh, honey." She touched his cheek, sniffling back a new wave of emotions. "I'm just glad you're okay." A tear slipped down her cheek before she could catch it.

"Don't cry and get all mushy, Mom."

A watery laugh escaped her. "It's what moms do best."

Jason caught sight of Devin and one side of his mouth hiked up in a groggy smile. "Uncle Devin," he rasped.

Devin moved closer and picked up Jason's unharmed hand. "Shh, Tiger. You need to rest and get better so we can take you home."

Jason's little fingers flexed around Devin's hand. "Take care of Mom for me," he said sleepily, his lashes lowering heavily over his eyes.

"I will," Devin promised, his heart expanding at the boy's concern for his mother, especially at a time like this.

Lilianne gave Jason another kiss and promised to be back soon, but the boy seemed to have fallen asleep. She wanted to linger, just to make sure he was truly okay, but Devin gently ushered her from the room, reminding her of the doctor's request to stay only a few minutes.

Devin drove her home. Emotionally exhausted, Lilianne closed her eyes, letting her head loll against the cool window. When Devin pulled into her driveway and cut the engine, he realized she was asleep. Leaving her for a moment, he unlocked the front door, turned on some lights, then came back for her. Lilianne's eyes blinked open when Devin scooped her up into his strong arms. Too tired to protest, she let him carry her into the house to her bedroom. No words were spoken as he placed her on the bed, took off her shoes and smoothed back the hair from her face.

"Sleep well," he said, smiling gently. "I'll call you in the morning."

Panic flowed through Lilianne's veins. She thought of Devin walking out of her life again, of all the pain and loneliness she felt without him. She didn't know if she could endure it anymore. Pride and independence weren't worth much if you weren't happy.

As Devin turned to leave, Lilianne grabbed his arm, halting him. He looked at her, but remained silent.

Lilianne swallowed the huge lump clogging her throat. "Don't leave me, Devin." Her voice cracked and tears misted her eyes. "I need you."

His dark eyes flickered with emotion, but he still didn't say a word. His body coiled up tight, hoping, waiting.

Sliding to the edge of the bed, she drew him near. He came unresistingly. "Almost losing Jason made me realize how precious life is. I don't want to waste it being lonely. My life is empty without you."

Devin pulled Lilianne up, wrapping her in his arms. He buried his face in the curve of her neck, breathing in her scent. "God, I've waited so long to hear you say that." Pulling back, he slid his hand along her jaw, using his thumb to tilt her chin up. He gazed into her eyes. "Staying away from you has been the hardest thing I've ever done. I've missed you so much, Lily. Your warmth, your smile, even your anger."

"Then marry me," she breathed. Her heart opened and rejoiced, knowing she'd made the right decision.

His smile held tenderness and promise. "Ahh, Lily, love, you just try and stop me." Then he kissed her softly on the lips.

Epilogue

Lilianne sucked in her breath as the little life in her belly did a somersault. "Did you feel that, Devin?" she asked, glancing over her shoulder at her husband. Devin sat behind her on the floor, his thighs on either side of her, his hand splayed on her round belly.

"He's got quite a kick," he said, grinning.

"I want to feel!" Jason jumped up from his position in front of the TV to kneel beside Lilianne and Devin. Placing his hands on her stomach, he waited impatiently for the baby to move. Finally it happened again, and Jason looked up, his eyes wide. Delighted laughter spilled from his lips.

"What's going on?" Elizabeth asked, walking into the room, followed by Emily.

"Want to feel the baby move?" Devin asked, slipping his palms lower to make room for two more hands.

"Yeah!" Emily and Elizabeth said simultaneously, rushing to Lilianne's side. They both found a spot on her stomach and waited expectantly.

Just as Lilianne was going to announce that the baby had probably fallen asleep, a foot or elbow—she couldn't tell which—was dragged across the largest part of her distended belly.

"Wow!" Elizabeth said.

"Radical!" Emily said.

Jason giggled.

Lilianne leaned into Devin, thinking she'd never felt so blissfuly happy and secure. She looked at the hands touching her belly, all the life and love each touch radiated to the baby within. Smiling, Lilianne realized how truly blessed she was. She had three beautiful children, another on the way, a thriving career—and the love of a man who made her life whole and complete.

What more could a woman ask for?

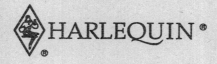

Relive the romance...
Harlequin and Silhouette
are proud to present

A program of collections of three complete novels by the most requested
authors with the most requested themes. Be sure to look for one volume each
month with three complete novels by top name authors.

In January: **WESTERN LOVING**   Susan Fox
                                  JoAnn Ross
                                  Barbara Kaye

Loving a cowboy is easy—taming him isn't!

In February: **LOVER, COME BACK!**   Diana Palmer
                                      Lisa Jackson
                                      Patricia Gardner Evans

It was over so long ago—yet now they're calling, "Lover, Come Back!"

In March: **TEMPERATURE RISING**   JoAnn Ross
                                    Tess Gerritsen
                                    Jacqueline Diamond

Falling in love—just what the doctor ordered!

Available at your favorite retail outlet.

REQ-G3

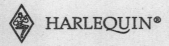

STOCK UP ON STOCKING STUFFERS
AND GET A FREE ROMANCE NOVEL

Collect all six STOCKING STUFFERS this December and receive a romance novel free—yours to enjoy when you have a few stolen moments to call your own. Once this special holiday season is over, take some time out to enjoy a longer-length romance novel from the romance experts—Harlequin and Silhouette—yours free when you collect all six proofs of purchase.

One proof of purchase can be found in the back pages of each STOLEN MOMENTS title this December.

To receive your gift, please fill out the information below and mail six (6) original proof-of-purchase coupons from December STOLEN MOMENTS titles, plus $1.00 for postage and handling (check or money order—do not send cash), payable to Harlequin Books, to: IN THE U.S.: P.O. Box 9071, Buffalo, NY, 14269-9071; IN CANADA: P.O. Box 604, Fort Erie, Ontario, L2A 5X3.

NAME: _____

ADDRESS: _____

_____

CITY: _____

STATE/PROVINCE: _____

ZIP/POSTAL CODE: _____

ONE PROOF OF PURCHASE 078 KBQ

Requests must be received by February 28, 1994.
Please allow 4–6 weeks after receipt of order for delivery.

HARLEQUIN • *Silhouette*